one night
that changes everything

ALSO BY
LAUREN BARNHOLDT

Two-way Street

Watch Me

Sometimes It Happens

one night

that changes everything

LAUREN BARNHOLDT

Simon Pulse

New York London Toronto Sydney

SIMON PULSE

An imprint of Simon & Schuster Children's Publishing Division
1230 Avenue of the Americas, New York, NY 10020
First Simon Pulse paperback edition June 2011
Copyright © 2010 by Lauren Barnholdt
All rights reserved, including the right of reproduction
in whole or in part in any form.
SIMON PULSE and colophon are registered trademarks of Simon & Schuster, Inc.
Also available in a Simon Pulse hardcover edition.
For information about special discounts for bulk purchases,
please contact Simon & Schuster Special Sales at 1-866-506-1949
or business@simonandschuster.com.
The Simon & Schuster Speakers Bureau can bring authors to your live event.
For more information or to book an event contact the Simon & Schuster Speakers
Bureau at 1-866-248-3049 or visit our website at www.simonspeakers.com.
Designed by Mike Rosamilia
The text of this book was set in Cochin.
Manufactured in the United States of America
2 4 6 8 10 9 7 5 3
The Library of Congress has cataloged the hardcover edition as follows:
Barnholdt, Lauren.
One night that changes everything / by Lauren Barnholdt.—1st Simon Pulse
hardcover ed.
p. cm.
Summary: A shy high school junior spends a madcap night trying to
retrieve her private notebook from a vengeful ex-boyfriend.
ISBN 978-1-4169-9479-4 (hc)
[1. Dating (Social customs)—Fiction. 2. Revenge—Fiction. 3. Diaries—Fiction.]
I. Title.
PZ7.B2667On 2010
[Fic]—dc22
2009041828
ISBN 978-1-4442-0367-3 (pbk)
ISBN 978-1-4169-9480-0 (eBook)

For Aaron, who came into my life
and changed everything

Acknowledgments

Thank you, thank you, thank you to:

Jen Klonsky, editor extraordinaire, for her awesome editorial suggestions, and for believing in this book from the beginning

Alyssa Eisner Henkin, the best agent a girl could ask for

Kelsey and Krissi, for being amazing sisters

My mom, for always believing in me no matter what

My dad, for reading everything I've ever written

Jodi Yanarella, Scott Neumyer, Kevin Cregg, and the Gorvine family for all their support

Jessica Burkhart for being a fabulous NYC buddy, and the other half of Team Barnhart

Mandy Hubbard, for answering all my venting emails and for Text in the City

And last but not least, to everyone who read *Two-way Street* and sent me e-mails letting me know how much you loved it — it means more than you know . . .

one night
that changes everything

Chapter One

7:00 p.m.

I lose everything. Keys, my wallet, money, library books.
People don't even take it seriously anymore. Like when I lost
the hundred dollars my grandma gave me for back-to-school
shopping, my mom didn't blink an eye. She was all, "Oh,
Eliza, you should have given it to me to hold on to" and then
she just went on with her day.

I try not to really stress out about it anymore. I mean,
the things I lose eventually show up. And if they don't, I can
always replace them.

Except for my purple notebook. My purple notebook is
completely and totally irreplaceable. It's not like I can just
march into the Apple store and buy another one. Which is
why it totally figures that after five years of keeping very close

tabs on it (Five years! I've never done anything consistently for five years!) I've lost it.

"What are you doing?" my best friend Clarice asks. She's sitting at my computer in the corner of my room, IMing with her cousin Jamie. Clarice showed up at nine o'clock this morning, with a huge bag of Cheetos and a six-pack of soda. "I'm ready to party," she announced when I opened my front door. Then she pushed past me and marched up to my room.

I tried to point out that it was way too early to be up on a Saturday, but Clarice didn't care because: (a) she's a morning person and (b) she thought the weekend needed to start asap, since my parents are away for the night, and she figured we should maximize the thirty-six-hour window of their absence.

"I'm looking for something," I say from under my bed. My body is shoved halfway under, rooting around through the clothes, papers, and books that have somehow accumulated under there since the last time I cleaned. Which was, you know, months ago. My hand brushes against something wet and hard. Hmm.

"What could you possibly be looking for?" she asks. "We have everything we need right here."

"If you're referring to the Cheetos," I say, "I'm sorry, but I think I'm going to need a little more than that."

"No one," Clarice declares, "needs more than Cheetos." She takes one out of the bag and slides it into her mouth, chewing delicately. Clarice is from the South, and for some reason, when she moved here a couple of years ago, she'd never had

Cheetos. We totally bonded over them one day in the cafeteria, and ever since then, we've been inseparable. Me, Clarice, and Cheetos. Not necessarily in that order.

"So what are you looking for?" she asks again.

"Just my notebook," I say. "The purple one."

"Oooh," she says. "Is that your science notebook?"

"No," I say.

"Math?" she tries.

"No," I say.

"Then what?"

"It's just this notebook I need," I say. I abandon the wet, hard mystery object under the bed, deciding I can deal with it later. And by later, I mean, you know, never.

"What kind of notebook?" she presses.

"Just, you know, a notebook," I lie. My face gets hot, and I hurry over to my closet and open the door, turning my back to her so that she can't see I'm getting all flushed.

The thing is, no one really knows the truth about what's in my purple notebook. Not Clarice, not my other best friend, Marissa, not even my sister, Kate. The whole thing is just way too embarrassing. I mean, a notebook that lists every thing that you're afraid of doing? Like, written down? In *ink*? Who does that? It might be a little bit crazy, even. Like, for real crazy. Not just "oh isn't that charming and endearing" crazy but "wow that might be a deep-seated psychological issue" crazy.

But I started the notebook when I was twelve, so I figure

I have a little bit of wiggle room in the psychiatric disorders department. And besides, it was totally started under duress. There was this whole situation, this very real possibility that my dad was going to get a job transfer to a town fifty miles away. My whole family was going to move to a place where no one knew us.

So of course in my deluded little twelve-year-old brain, I became convinced that if I could just move to a different house and a different town, I'd be a totally different person. I'd leave my braces and frizzy hair behind, and turn myself into a goddess. No one would know me at my new school, so I could be anyone I wanted, not just "Kate Sellman's little sister, Eliza." I bought a purple notebook at the drugstore with my allowance, and I started writing down all the things I was afraid to do at the time, but would of course be able to do in my new school.

They were actually pretty lame at first, like French kiss a boy, or ask a boy to the dance, or wear these ridiculous tight pants that all the girls were wearing that year. But somehow putting them down on paper made me feel better, and after my dad's job transfer fell through, I kept writing in it. And writing in it, and writing in it, and writing in it. And, um, I still write in it. Not every day or anything. Just occasionally.

Of course, the things I list have morphed a little over the years from silly to serious. I still put dumb things in, like wanting to wear a certain outfit, but I have more complicated things in there too. Like how I wish I had the nerve to go to a political rally, or how I wish I could feel okay about not knowing what I want to major in when I go to college. And the fact that these very embarrassing and current things are WRITTEN DOWN IN MY NOTEBOOK means I have to find it. Like, now.

The doorbell rings as I'm debating whether or not the notebook could be in my parents' car, traveling merrily on its way to the antique furniture conference they went to. This would be good, since (a) it would at least be safe, but bad because (a) what if my parents read it and (b) I won't be able to check the car until they get home, which means I will spend the entire weekend on edge and freaking out.

"That's probably Marissa," I say to Clarice.

Clarice groans and rolls her blue eyes. "Why is *she* coming over?" she asks. She pouts out her pink-glossed bottom lip.

"Because she's our friend," I say. Which is only a half truth. Marissa is my friend, and Clarice is my friend, and Marissa and Clarice . . . well . . . they have this weird sort of love/hate relationship. They both really love each other deep down (at least, I think they do), but Marissa thinks Clarice is a little bit of an airhead and kind of a tease, and Clarice thinks Marissa is a little crazy and slightly slutty. They're both kind of right.

Marissa must have gotten tired of waiting and just let herself in, because a second later she appears in my doorway.

"What are you doing in there?" she asks.

"I'm looking for something," I say from inside my closet, where I'm throwing bags, sweaters, belts, and shoes over my shoulder in an effort to see if my notebook has somehow been

5

buried at the bottom. I try to remember the last time I wrote in it. I think it was last week. I had dinner with my sister and then I wrote about what I would say to . . . Well. What I would say to a certain person. If I had the guts to, I mean. And if I ever wanted to even think or talk about that person again, which I totally don't.

"What something?" Marissa asks. She steps gingerly through the disaster area that is now my room and plops down on the bed.

"A notebook," Clarice says. Her fingers are flying over the keyboard of my laptop as she IMs.

"You mean like for school?" Marissa asks. "You said this was going to be our party weekend! No studying allowed!"

"Yeah!" Clarice says, agreeing with Marissa for once. She holds the bag out to her. "You want a Cheeto?" Marissa takes one.

"No," I say, "*You guys* said this was going to be our party weekend." Although, honestly, we don't really party all that much. At least, I don't. "All I said was, 'My parents are going away on Saturday, do you want to come over and keep me company?'"

"Yes," Clarice says. "And that implies party weekend."

"Yeah," Marissa says. "Come on, Eliza, we have to at least do *something*."

"Like what?" I ask.

"Like invite some guys over," Clarice says.

Marissa nods in agreement, then adds, "And go skinny dipping and get drunk."

And then Clarice gets a super-nervous look on her face, and she quickly rushes on to add, "I mean, not *guys* guys. I mean, not guys to like date or anything. Just to . . . I mean, I don't know if you're ready to, or if you even want to—oh, crap, Eliza, I'm sorry." She bites her lip, and Marissa shoots her a death glare, her brown eyes boring into Clarice's blue ones.

"It's fine," I say. "You guys don't have to keep tiptoeing around it. I am completely and totally over him." I'm totally lying, and they totally know it. The thing is, three and a half weeks ago, I got dumped by Cooper Marriatti, *a.k.a.* the last person I wrote about in my notebook, *a.k.a.* the person who I never, ever want to talk about again. (Obviously I can say his name while defending myself from the allegation that I still like him—that is a total exception to the "never bring his name up again" rule.) I really liked him, but it didn't work out. To put it mildly. Cooper did something really despicable to me, and for that reason, I am totally over it.

"Of course you are," Clarice says, nodding her head up and down. "And of course I know we don't have to tiptoe around it."

"I heard he didn't get into Brown," Marissa announces. I snap my head up and step out of my closet, interested in spite of myself.

"What do you mean?" I ask. Cooper is a senior, a year older than us, and his big dream was to get into Brown. Seriously, it was all his family could talk about. It was pretty annoying, actually, now that I think about it. I mean, I don't think he even really *wanted* to go to Brown. He just applied because his parents wanted him to, and the only reason *they* even wanted him to go was because his dad went there, and his grandpa went there, and maybe even his great-grandpa went there. If Brown was even around then. Anyway, the point is, the fact that he didn't get in is a big deal. To him and his family, I mean. Obviously, I could care less.

"Yeah," Marissa says. "Isabella Royce told me." She quickly averts her eyes. Ugh. Isabella Royce. She's the girl Cooper is now rumored to be dating, this totally ridiculous sophomore. She's very exotic-looking with long, straight dark hair, perfect almond-shaped eyes, and dark skin. I hate her.

"Anyway," I say.

"Yeah, anyway," Clarice says. She holds out the bag of Cheetos, and this time I take one. "Oooh," she says as I crunch away. "Looks like Jeremiah added some new Facebook pictures." She leans over and squints at the screen of my laptop. She's saying this just to mess with Marissa. Jeremiah is the guy Marissa likes. They hook up once in a while, and it's kind of a . . . I guess you would say, booty-call situation. Meaning that, you know, Jeremiah calls her when he wants to hook up, and Marissa keeps waiting for it to turn into something else.

"That's nice," Marissa says, trying to pretend she doesn't care. "Here," she says, picking a stack of letters up off the bed and holding them out to me. "I brought you your mail."

"Thanks," I say, flipping through it aimlessly. I hardly ever get mail, but sometimes my sister, Kate, will get a catalog or something sent to her, and since she's away at college, I can hijack it. But today there actually is a letter for me. Well, to me and my parents. It's from the school.

"What's that?" Marissa asks, noticing me looking at it. She's off the bed now and over in the corner, picking through the mound of clothes I hefted out of my closet. She picks a shirt off the pile on the floor, holds it in front of herself, and studies her reflection in the full-length mirror. "Are my boobs crooked?" she asks suddenly. She grabs them and pushes them together through her shirt. "I think maybe my boobs are crooked."

"Your boobs," I say, rolling my eyes, "are not crooked." Clarice stays noticeably quiet and Marissa frowns.

"They're definitely crooked," Marissa says. I slide my finger under the envelope flap and pull out the piece of paper.

"You should really hope that's not true," Clarice says sagely. She whirls around on my desk chair and studies Marissa.

"Why not?" Marissa asks.

"Because there's no way to really correct that," Clarice says. "Like, if your boobs are too big, you can get them reduced; if they're too droopy, you can get them lifted. But for crooked boobs, I dunno." She looks really worried, like Marissa's crooked boobs might mean the end of her. "Although I guess maybe you could get them, like, balanced or something." She grins, totally proud of herself for coming up with this idea.

"Hmm," Marissa says. She smoothes her long brown

hair back from her face. "You're right. There's no, like, boob-straightening operation."

"You guys," I say, "are nuts." I look down at the folded piece of paper in my hand, which is probably some kind of invitation to Meet-the-Teacher-Night or something.

Dear Eliza, Mr. and Mrs. Sellman,

This letter is to advise you that we will be having a preliminary hearing on Tuesday, November 17, at 2:00 p.m., to discuss Eliza's response to the recent slander complaint that has been filed against her. Eliza will be called on to talk about her experience with the website LanesboroLosers.com including her involvement and participation in the comments that were posted on October 21, about a student, Cooper Marriatti.

Please be advised that all of you will be allowed to speak.

If you have any questions, please feel free to give me a call at 555-0189, ext. 541.

Sincerely,
Graham Myers, Dean of Students

Oh. My. God.

"What the hell," I say, "is this?" I start waving the paper

around, flapping it back and forth in the air, not unlike the way a crazy person might do.

"What the hell is what?" Marissa asks. She drops her boobs, crosses the room in two strides, and plucks the paper out of my hand. She scans it, then looks at Clarice.

"Oh," she says. Clarice jumps up off her perch at my desk and takes the paper from Marissa. She reads it, and then Clarice and Marissa exchange a look. One of those looks you never, ever want to see your best friends exchanging. One of those, "Uh-oh, we have a secret and do we really want to tell her?" looks.

"What?" I demand. I narrow my eyes at the both of them. "What do you two know about this?"

Marissa bites her lip. "Wel-l-l-l," she says. "I'm not sure if it's true."

"Not sure if what's true?" I say.

"It's nothing," Clarice says. She gives Marissa another look, one that says, "Let's not tell her, we're going to freak her out too much."

"Totally," Marissa says. "It's nothing."

"Someone," I say, "had better tell me exactly what this nothing is." I put my hands on my hips and try to look menacing.

"I heard it from Marissa," Clarice says, sounding nervous.

"I heard it from Kelsey Marshall," Marissa says.

"HEARD WHAT?" I almost scream. I mean, honestly.

"Wel-l-l-l," Marissa says again. "The rumor is that Cooper

didn't get into Brown because of what you wrote about him on Lanesboro Losers."

"But that's . . . that doesn't make any sense." I frown, and Marissa and Clarice exchange another disconcerting look.

Lanesboro Losers is a website that my older sister, Kate, started last year when she was a senior. The concept is simple: Every guy in our school is listed and has a profile. Kind of like Facebook, except Kate set up profiles for every guy—so basically they're on there, whether they like it or not. Under each guy's picture is a place for people to leave comments with information they may have about that guy and how he is when it comes to girls.

So, like, for example—if you date a guy and then you find out he has a girlfriend who goes to another school, you can log on, find his profile, and write, "You should be careful about this guy since the ass has a girlfriend who goes to another school."

It's pretty genius when you think about it. Kate got the idea when a bunch of the boys at our school started this list ranking the hottest girls in school. Only it wasn't just like "the top eight hottest girls" or whatever. They ranked them all the way down to the very last one. Kate, who was number 1 on the list, was outraged. So she decided to fight back and started Lanesboro Losers. Even though she's at college now, she keeps up with the hosting and has a bunch of girls from our school acting as moderators. (I would totally be a moderator if I could, but again, another thing I'm afraid of—the moderators take a certain amount of abuse at school from the guys who know what they do.)

"What do you mean he didn't get into Brown because of what I wrote about him?" I ask now, mulling this new information over in my head.

"He didn't get into Brown because of what you wrote about him," Marissa repeats.

"I heard you the first time," I say. "But that makes zero sense."

"It totally makes sense," Clarice says. "Apparently the Brown recruiter Googled him, and when they read what you wrote about his math test, they brought it up at his interview and basically told him his early decision application was getting rejected."

I sit down on the bed. "That thing I wrote about his math test was true," I say defensively.

Well. Sort of. Last year before his math final, Cooper got a bunch of study questions from his friend Tyler, and when he showed up to take the test, it turned out they weren't just study questions—it was the actual test. Cooper had already given the packet back to Tyler, and for some ridiculous reason, he didn't want to get Tyler into trouble, so he didn't tell anyone. So see? He *did* cheat, even though it was unintentional.

"It was totally true," Marissa says, nodding up and down. "Which is why you shouldn't feel bad about what you wrote." She gives Clarice a pointed look.

"Totally," Clarice says. "You shouldn't feel bad about it."

She keeps nodding her head up and down, the way people do when they don't really believe what they're saying.

I close my eyes, lean back on my bed, and think about what I wrote about Cooper on Lanesboro Losers. I have pretty much every word memorized, since I spent a couple of hours obsessing over what I should write. (It couldn't be too bitter, but it couldn't look like I was trying *not* to be too bitter either. It was a very delicate balance that needed to be struck. Also, I couldn't post the truth about what really happened between me and Cooper, since it was way too humiliating.) I finally settled on, "Cooper Marriatti is a total and complete jerk. He cheated on his final math test junior year just so he could pass, and he also might have herpes." The herpes thing was of course made up, but I couldn't help myself. (And, as you can see, despite my best efforts, I totally missed the balance.)

Anyway, the thing about Lanesboro Losers is that once you post something on there, they won't take it down. It's a fail-safe, just in case you end up posting something about a guy when he's being a jerk to you and then try to log on and erase it when you guys are back together. Kate set it up so that it's totally not allowed.

"Whatever," I say, my heart beating fast. "I don't feel bad." I hope saying the words out loud will make them true. And for a second, it works. I mean, who cares about dumb Cooper and dumb Brown? It's his own fault. If he hadn't done something totally disgusting and despicable to me, if he hadn't lied to me and been a complete and total jerk, I wouldn't have written that, and he would be going to Brown. So it's totally his own fault, and if he wants to blame anyone, he should blame himself, really, because it's no concern to me if he wants to—

My cell phone starts ringing then, and I claw through the blankets on my bed, looking for it. Some books clatter onto the floor, and Clarice jumps back. She's wearing open-toed silver sparkly shoes, and one of the books comes dangerously close to falling on her foot.

"Hello," I say. The number on the caller ID is one I don't recognize, so I try to sound super-professional and innocent, just in case it's someone from the dean's office.

There's a commotion on the other end, something that sounds like voices and music, then the sound of something crinkling, and then finally, I hear a male voice say, "Eliza?"

"Yeah?" I say.

"Eliza, listen, I didn't . . ." Whoever it is is keeping their voice really low and quiet, and I'm having a lot of trouble hearing what they're saying.

"Hello!" I repeat.

"Who is it?" Marissa asks. "Is it Jeremiah?" Sometimes Jeremiah calls me looking for Marissa, if he thinks we might be together, or if he can't get through to her for some reason. Clarice's theory is that he does this so he can relay messages to me instructing Marissa to come over for a hookup, while not having to actually talk to her.

"Hello?" I say again into the phone. I put my finger in my

other ear the way they do sometimes on TV, and it seems to help a little.

"Eliza, it's me," the voice says, and this time I hear it loud and clear. Cooper. "Eliza, you have to listen to me, the 318s and Tyler . . ." There's a burst of static, and the rest of what he's saying gets cut off.

"Cooper?" I ask, and my heart starts to beat a little faster.

Marissa and Clarice look at each other. Then in one fast springlike movement, they're on the bed next to me, huddled around the phone.

"Yeah, it's me," he says. There's another burst of commotion on the other end of the line.

"Eliza, listen to me . . ." he says. "You're going to have to—" And then I hear him talking to someone else in the background.

"What do you want?" I ask, my stomach dropping into my shoes. "If this is about you not getting into Brown, then honestly, I don't even care. It's all your own fault that you didn't get into Brown, and I don't regret—"

"Eliza," Cooper says. "Listen. To. Me. You have to meet me." His voice is low now, serious and dark. "Right now. At Cure."

Marissa and Clarice are falling all over themselves and me, trying to get at the phone, and Clarice's earring gets caught on my sweater. "OW, OW, MY EAR!" she screams, then reaches down and sets it free. I pull the phone away from my ear and put it on speaker in an effort to get them to calm down.

"Cure?" I repeat to Cooper incredulously. Cure is a night-club in Boston, and they're notorious for not IDing. I've never been there. But Kate used to go all the time, and most of the kids at my school have gone at least once or twice.

"Yeah," he says. "Eliza . . ." I hear someone say something to him in the background, and then suddenly his tone changes. "Meet me there. At Cure. In an hour."

"Tell him no," Marissa whispers, her brown eyes flashing. "Tell him that you never want to see him again!"

"Ask him if he really turned you in to the dean's office!" Clarice says. She picks up the letter from the dean's office and waves it in the air in front of me.

"Are you there?" Cooper asks, all snottylike.

"Yes, I'm here," I say. "Look, why do you want to meet me at Cure?"

"Don't ask questions," he says. "You'll find out when you get there. And make sure you wear something sexy."

I pull the phone away from my ear and look at it for a sec-ond, sure I've misheard him. "*'Wear something sexy'?* Are you *crazy?*" I ask. "I'm not going." This doesn't sound like a "Come to Cure so I can apologize to you and make sure you forgive me for the horrible things I've done" kind of request. It sounds like a "Come to Cure so that something horrible can happen that may involve humiliating you further."

Marissa nods her head and gives me a "You go, girl" look.

"Yes, you are," Cooper says.

"No, I'm not," I say.

"Yes, you are," Cooper says. And then he says something horrible. Something I wouldn't ever even imagine he would say in a million years. Something that is maybe quite possibly the worst thing he could ever say ever, ever, *ever.* "Because I have your purple notebook." And then he hangs up.

Chapter Two

7:37 p.m.

"What the hell is in the damn thing?" Marissa asks. The three of us have piled into Marissa's car and are on the Mass Pike traveling at about eighty miles an hour. Usually I'm not a fan of Marissa (or anyone, really) driving that fast, but at this point, speed is the least of my worries. My first being, you know, that Cooper has my notebook, and the second being that I am on my way to Cure, and that I am wearing a ridiculous outfit.

"It's just . . . I need it, okay?" I'm rummaging through my purse for my Passion Pink lip gloss. I slide the visor mirror down and smear the gloss on. Just because my life is potentially over doesn't mean I don't want to look good. Plus I'm going to see Cooper, and even if he is a total bastard, I might as well look my best when I see him. Not that I care about Cooper, of course. But there will be other guys there too. Guys that might potentially be my future husband.

Plus, lipstick goes with this outfit, which consists of:

- tight skinny leg jeans
- gray shoes with platform heels and studs on the sides
- a backless silver shirt that plunges down so far in front I'm afraid my boobs are going to fall out

All of these items were left in my sister Kate's closet when she left for college. Marissa insisted I wear them, since apparently nothing I owned was Cure-appropriate.

"Why are you putting lipstick on?" Clarice pipes up from the backseat. One of the good things about Clarice and Marissa having their little rivalry is that I always get to ride shotgun.

"Because we're going to a club," I say. I glance in the backseat. "You're wearing lipstick," I point out. Of course, this isn't really the same thing. Clarice always wears lipstick. She's mostly always dressed up. I think it's part of her Southern upbringing. Like right now, for example. She's wearing a sleeveless long white eyelet shirt over black leggings and delicate silver open-toed sandals. Her long blond hair is curled perfectly, and her makeup is flawless. This is how she showed up at my house this morning. At 9:00 a.m. When most normal people are dead to the world.

"Yeah," Clarice says. "But I already had my lipstick on. You're putting yours on now, like you're getting ready for the club."

"We are going to a club," I repeat. "There's nothing wrong with putting on makeup before we get to a club."

"It's because of Cooper, isn't it?" Clarice asks. She flops back into the seat, her long blond curls bouncing. I'm not sure if it's my imagination, but she almost seems . . . *happy* about it. That I might be dressing up for Cooper. Which would kind of make sense. Clarice is an eternal romantic, and she gets very caught up in the idea of people getting back together. Plus she always loved Cooper. I glare at her.

"Whatever," Marissa says. She signals and changes lanes. "Are you going to tell us what's in this notebook or what? That was part of the deal, remember?"

It took me a while to convince Marissa that we needed to go to Cure. One, she's not really supposed to be driving her car into the city. Two, she didn't understand why I was in such a rush to go off and meet Cooper. Which makes sense, given everything that he's done to me. The only way I could get her to take me was to promise to tell her what was in the notebook.

"Look," I say, taking a deep breath. "We are going to Cure, I am going to get the notebook back, and maybe then I will tell you what's in it."

"So I'm just supposed to take you down there, without any idea what's going on?"

"Um, it's called having faith in your friends, Marissa," Clarice says from the backseat. She's opened a bottle of nail polish and is painting her toenails a dark crimson color.

"Thank you, Clarice," I say.

"Oh, I have faith in my friends, all right," Marissa says. She pushes her bangs out of her face, and pulls the car onto the off-ramp. "But I also like to know what they're doing so that I can watch out for them." She glances in the rearview mirror and tries to catch Clarice's eye, but she's too busy with her nail polish. "You'd better not spill that," she says. "My mom will kill me if my car gets messed up, and then I'll kill you."

"You won't be able to kill me if you're dead," Clarice says sweetly. "And besides, I'm not going to spill it. I'm very good with balancing things." She rolls her eyes like she can't even fathom the possibility of spilling her nail polish, just as Marissa goes over a pothole, and the bottle almost drops onto the floor.

"Oops!" Clarice says holding it up triumphantly. "Close one."

When we get to Cure, we breeze right by the bouncer without any sort of ID check, and once we're inside, I become instantly grateful I took the time to change. Even though it's mid-November and forty degrees outside, everyone in here is scantily clad. Most of the girls are in tight black pants or short skirts, with low-cut tops. In fact, it seems like the more skin and/or tightness, the better.

Marissa, Clarice, and I huddle in a corner and look around for Cooper.

"Do you see him?" Marissa asks, as we all scan the crowd. Dance music is pumping through the speakers at a ridiculously high volume, but no one's really on the dance floor yet, and the tables set up around the perimeter of the club are mostly empty. At the bar, two guys are ordering drinks, and the bartender, a short girl with a lip piercing and a tight tank top, is laughing loudly at what they're saying. I guess it's too early for things to be really crazy in here.

"No," I say. "I don't think he's here."

"I'm going to get us some drinks and then we're going to wait for him," Clarice announces. She disappears and returns a few minutes later with two cosmopolitans (virgin for her — Clarice doesn't drink, so she always orders cranberry juice and then calls it a virgin cosmo) and a bottle of water wedged under her arm for Marissa, since she's driving. This doesn't seem like the kind of place in which one should order a cosmopolitan, but I can't really imagine Clarice ordering a rum and coke or a Bud Light or anything like that, and besides, I like cosmopolitans, so I'm not going to complain. We find a table in the middle section of the club, with a good view of the crowd, and sit down with our drinks.

"Now it's important to be haughty," Marissa is saying. "Don't let him think he's going to get one over on you." Hmm. That's great in theory, but I don't think Marissa really has a good grasp on what's in that notebook, a.k.a. all the information you'd possibly need to ruin my life.

I start to feel a little faint thinking about it, and so I take a big sip of my drink. It's cool and sweet going down, and I instantly feel better. Although I don't think drinking cosmos is going to be a very good long-term solution because (a) alcohol dehydrates you, which is not a good thing when you're already feeling light-headed, and (b) it's going to do me no good to be drunk, since I'm going to need all my wits about me to deal with Cooper.

Marissa pulls her cell phone out and sets it down on the table next to her.

Clarice gets a disapproving look on her face.

"Why are you looking at me like that?" Marissa asks.

"Because you're taking your phone out just so you can wait for Jeremiah to call."

"So?" Marissa asks. "Jeremiah is a guy I am dating; of course I'm going to wait for his call. There is nothing wrong with wanting to talk to the guy you are dating."

Clarice takes a dainty sip of her drink and doesn't say anything. Since Jeremiah and Marissa spend most of their time making out, their relationship goes against everything Clarice believes a true-to-life romance should be. (That's Clarice's term, by the way. Not mine. I would never say anything like "true-to-life romance." Especially since I'm not the best one to be speaking about any kind of romance, true-to-life or not.)

Marissa opens her mouth to say something else, like

maybe she's going to defend her relationship with Jeremiah, when I see him. Cooper. Sitting over in the corner at one of those big round booths. He's by himself, wearing a navy blue long-sleeved T-shirt, and he's sipping what looks like a soda, but if I know Cooper, there's definitely some rum in that drink. Or maybe even tequila. Actually, that's not true. Cooper's not really a big drinker. I mean, he drinks, but he's not one of those people who's always falling all over themselves drunk every weekend. But for some reason it's better if I assume he's over there with some hard liquor. It makes him seem shadier. Not that he really needs any help in that department.

"There he is," I say, cutting off Marissa as she's about to launch into a long spiel involving the reasons Jeremiah is not just using her for sex. My voice sounds all strained, like I'm trying to talk around a mouthful of marbles.

"What?" Clarice asks. She leans in closer and I raise my voice to be heard over the music.

"There. He. Is," I say. "Don't look." But of course the two of them do look, turning around on their swivel chairs until they're facing him. Cooper looks up and locks eyes with me, and I quickly look away.

"Oh. My. God," I say to Clarice and Marissa. "Is he . . . what is he doing, is he coming over here?"

"Um, no," Clarice says. "He's just . . ." she frowns, ". . . sitting."

"Is he with anyone else?" I ask. "Do you see Tyler? Or any of the 318s?" The 318s are this secret society at our school, a sort of high school fraternity composed of all the most popular (and jerkiest, IMO), guys at our school. No one knows exactly why they're called the 318s, although the rumor is that the original three founding members had had sex with eighteen girls between them, and they apparently thought it would be a real hoot to incorporate that into their name.

Anyway, no one's supposed to know who their members are, but it's pretty much common knowledge that Tyler Twill is their president. And once you know that, you can kind of figure out who's in by who's hanging out with him. Although of course they'd never admit it. But I happen to know for a fact that Cooper is one of their members. They're the ones who made him do the totally ridiculous, despicable thing that he did to me a few weeks ago. It was part of his initiation task.

"He seems like he's alone," Marissa says.

"Do you see my notebook anywhere?" I ask.

"Um, no," Marissa says. "I don't see a notebook anywhere. It could be on the seat next to him though."

"You think?"

"I don't know," Marissa says. "If this is some kind of game, then he definitely wouldn't bring it with him. Cooper Marriatti's a lot of things, but he's not stupid."

"Or ugly," Clarice says, sighing. I glare at her, even though she's, of course, right. Cooper isn't ugly. He's really hot. But still. So not the time to bring it up.

"First of all," I say, starting to feel angry. "He actually *is* kind of that stupid, because anyone who would get involved with the 318s cannot be that smart. And second of all, he really isn't even that cute." Lie, lie, lie. "Did I ever tell you about the scar on his stomach? He's totally deformed."

Clarice and Marissa go all quiet and look at each other nervously, because of course I've told them about the scar on Cooper's stomach and of course I've told them about how sexy it is.

He got it while he was snowmobiling and he fell off and the snowmobile RAN HIM OVER and Cooper didn't even go to the hospital until later when they found out he had internal injuries. Of course, it's totally possible that I just (used to) think the scar was sexy because of what we were doing the first time I saw it. I swallow around the lump in my throat.

"And furthermore," I say, "I really wish you two would stop looking at each other like that. It's kind of rude." I take another sip of my drink. A big sip. But whatever. What is it they call alcohol? Liquid courage? Good. Fine. I'll take all the courage I can get right now, liquid or otherwise. "I will be right back," I announce. And then I hop off my chair and march right over to where Cooper is sitting.

"Hey," Cooper says when he sees me. He doesn't even look nervous. In fact, he looks totally relaxed, his arms draped across the back of the huge booth he's sitting in. Doesn't he know that if you are alone, you're not supposed to take a big booth that is meant for larger parties? What a jerk. Also, why isn't he nervous? I could totally freak out on him if I wanted.

I would have a right to freak out on him, in fact, after what he did to me. I could . . . I don't know . . . punch him or scream at him or make a big scene, even.

"Give it back," I demand and hold my hand out. Maybe he'll get more nervous if he sees I'm bossing him around, that I am obviously a force to be reckoned with.

"I don't have it," Cooper says. He moves over in the booth, then pats the seat next to him and motions for me to sit down. I look over my shoulder to where Clarice and Marissa are sitting and then slide in next to him.

"So what's the deal?" I ask. "What is this about?" Our legs are touching underneath the table, and I want to pull mine away, but I don't. Not because I want to keep my leg against his, God no, but because I don't want to give him the satisfaction of pulling my leg away.

"Eliza," he says, leaning in close and whispering in my ear. His breath tickles my skin, and I can smell the familiar scent of Cooper—mint toothpaste and hair gel and some kind of yummy smelling cologne. "You're going to get your notebook back, but you're going to have to do what they say."

"Do what they say?" I look at him. "Do what *who* say?" Even though I of course already know who he's talking about.

"You know, Tyler and all of them." Cooper moves away from me then and looks at a spot across the room. I follow his gaze and see Tyler standing in the corner, huddled around a high-topped table with a bunch of his friends. Ugh. This is like my worst nightmare. I close my eyes and count to three, but when I open them, I'm still here.

"Look," I say. "If you think I'm going to participate in some weird, sick little game of yours, then you're wrong." I look him right in the eye. "I already did that, remember?" Cooper has the decency to look away then, at least. Probably because he knows it's true, and he can't really dispute the truth. I reach down and rub my leg. It's still tingling from where he was touching it.

Cooper's phone starts to go off then. A text message. He looks at the phone and then looks at me.

"You have to ask a guy here to dance," he says. He scans the crowd. "That one." He points to an extremely good-looking guy at the table across from us. He's blond and wearing a blue button-up shirt and khaki pants. Tan skin. Expensive look-ing haircut. Not someone I would ever ask to dance. Mostly because I would never ask anyone to dance, but if I did, it would definitely not be that guy.

"I'm not," I say, gritting my teeth. "Doing that."

"Then they're going to put your notebook online," he says.

I blink at him, positive I've heard him wrong. "They're going to put my notebook online?" What the fuck is wrong with these people? I mean, honestly. "What the fuck is wrong with these people?" I ask.

"They're pissed," he says. "That you posted that thing about me online and kept me from getting into Brown. Plus you outed me."

"Outted you?"

"Yeah, outted me. As being one of the 318s."

"Are you *kidding* me?"

Cooper shrugs, downs the rest of his drink, and then gets up and crosses the room over to where the 318s are sitting. I'm left sitting at the huge booth by myself. I look down at the seat, thinking that maybe, just maybe, Cooper did bring the notebook and maybe he left it by accident. But of course the seat is empty.

I make my way back to Clarice and Marissa, my head spinning from the warmth of the club and the buzz of the alcohol and the shock of what just happened.

"What did he say, what did he say?" Clarice asks. She's out of her seat and jumping around, hopping back and forth from one foot to the other, back and forth on her high silver sandals.

"He said," I say, "that I have to ask that guy to dance."

"What guy?" Marissa asks. I point him out.

"Oooh, he's cute," Clarice says. "Lucky girl."

"That doesn't make sense," Marissa says, obviously a little quicker on the uptake than Clarice. "Why would they ask you to ask that guy to dance?"

"I don't know," I say, staring at him. "Maybe he's a crazy stalker or something, and they know if I ask him to dance, I'll end up in a dumpster somewhere, killed and dismembered."

But as soon as the words are out of my mouth, I realize that's not the reason. And that's because I remember something. Something from my purple notebook. Something I wrote last year, one night after Kate came home from Cure and it seemed like she had a really, really fun time. And that was, "Show up at Cure in a sexy outfit and ask the hottest guy there to dance."

And then I get it. The 318s have somehow decided to make me do the things that are in my notebook. All the things I'm afraid of. The things I've been writing since the seventh grade. And if I don't, they're going to post the notebook online, and everyone at school, no, everyone with an *Internet connection*, will know all my secrets. For a second, it feels like my throat swallows up my heart, and my breath catches in my chest. There's only one thing left to do. I put my head in my hands and start to cry.

Chapter Three

8:03 p.m.

This whole thing is pretty much my own fault. I mean, if I hadn't been stupid enough to think that Cooper Marriatti really wanted to date me, then I wouldn't be in this mess. But when he showed up at my work that day, he looked so cute and he seemed so nice and I guess I wanted to believe it so badly and so I did.

I work part-time at a paintball park, so it wasn't like I'd never had a hot guy come in before. In fact, it seemed like all we got there were hot guys. Of course most of them didn't pay any attention to me, and a lot of them had, you know, rage problems which is why they were there playing paintball in the first place.

But something about Cooper was different. The way he

leaned against the front counter and talked to me, the way he asked me tons of questions about paintball even when it became obvious that he already knew what he was doing.

Of course I knew who Cooper was—but I'd never actually paid much attention to him. He was the guy other girls drooled over, the kind of guy who'd go for my sister, Kate. I never really let myself crush too much on guys like that—they were to be admired from afar, like a painting or an actor on TV.

After Cooper played a round of paintball, he came back into the shop and spent the day with me, talking and laughing and getting me sodas from the snack bar. And when he asked me what time I got off work and if I wanted to hang out, I said yes. So he took me out to dinner and even walked me to my door when he dropped me off. The next morning at school, he was waiting for me at my locker.

It was only six weeks later, when I started getting in my head a little bit, that I decided to go through his stuff one day when we were at his house, studying. It wasn't my fault that I was going crazy. It was everyone else's. I could tell people at school couldn't figure out how someone like me ended up with Cooper Marriatti. And it made me all paranoid.

So Cooper was downstairs getting a drink of water or something, and I was supposed to be working on my history homework, but instead I decided to try and break into his e-mail, and when I couldn't figure that out, I went the old-fashioned way and just started going through his drawers.

And that's when I found it. The 318s' initiation sheet outlining how Cooper was dating me as his initiation task. He was getting all these points for doing certain things with me, like kissing me was five points, etc. And when he got to a certain number of points, he was in.

I freaked and yelled and screamed and Cooper tried to calm me down, but I wouldn't listen. I stormed out of his house, telling myself I would never talk to him again, but hoping he would at least try to call me. He didn't. That was three and a half weeks ago, and until tonight, we haven't talked.

"I am so stupid," I moan to Clarice and Marissa now. I mean, really. I'm in the National Honor Society for God's sake; how could this happen to me? Not to mention that I totally should have learned my lesson about losing things. Although. Now that I think about it. I think my purple notebook was in my locker. They probably broke into my locker and TOOK IT.

"No, you're not," Marissa says. "You were just a victim of the blatant misogynistic and ridiculous hierarchy that is high school in contemporary society. You have to take the power back."

"Okay, I'm not really sure what that means," Clarice says. She frowns and looks at Marissa. "Can you just say it in English please? Because honestly, it's not—"

Suddenly, Marissa cuts her off. "Ohmigod," she says, grabbing my arm. "OH. MY. GOD."

"What?" I say. "Ow, you're hurting my arm." I wipe the

tears off my face with the back of my hand and straighten up, trying to pry her fingers off of me.

"It's Jeremiah," she says. "JEREMIAH IS AT THIS CLUB."

"Okay," I say. Ow, ow, ow. Her fingers are digging into my arm and, hello, it hurts.

"He is over there with Julia Concord, what is he *doing* with Julia Concord?"

"I think y'all probably know the answer to that," Clarice says, because, you know, Julia Concord is kind of . . . well, let's just say she doesn't discriminate when it comes to hooking up. One time last year they found her giving some guy a blow job during a pep rally. They weren't even trying to be that discreet about it either. They were totally just under the bleachers, going at it.

"That jerk!" Marissa yells, slamming her fist on the table.

"Talk about a misogynistic hierarchy," Clarice says. She's texting on her phone, her fingers flying over the keyboard. "It's exactly what I've been trying to tell you. Guys will do anything they can to make you think they're with you, and then they will run off and hook up with whoever and whatever they can get their hands on. That's why it's so important not to give it up." She smiles, proud of herself.

Okay, we are really starting to get offtrack. The issue of the night is me, my notebook, and Cooper. Not Marissa and Jeremiah. Or Clarice and her views on teasing guys in an effort to make them fall in love with you.

"Hello!" I say. "Can we please focus here? I need to know more about taking the power back, like you said." I hear the desperation in my own voice. "Please, seriously, I need to take the power back, HELP ME TO GET THE POWER BACK!" A couple of girls at the table next to us turn around to look. But honestly, who cares? I have bigger problems than what two randoms in tight shirts think of me.

"Okay, LOOK," Marissa says. She spins my chair around until I'm facing her. "This whole secrecy thing is all well and good, but if you really expect us to help you, you have to tell us what is in the. God. Damn. Notebook."

I take a deep breath and look down at my hands. "It's just . . . it's this list." Then I look up and force myself to give them both my most dazzling smile, hoping this will suffice.

"List?" Clarice asks, her perfectly plucked eyebrows shooting up in interest. "Like of all the guys you'd hook up with if you weren't worried about people calling you a slut?" Marissa and I stare at her. "Not that I have one of those or anything." She studies her new pedicure. "I'm just saying that people could make one of those. Just in case."

"No, it's not about guys I want to have sex with. But it is a list." I give them another smile.

"You already said that," Marissa points out. She's starting to look annoyed.

"Yeah, we get it, it's a list," Clarice says. "What kind of list though?"

"It's this . . . list . . . ," I say, "of everything I'm afraid to do.

Of things I was going to do, that I am going to do, that I would do if . . ."

"If what?" Clarice prods.

"If I wasn't afraid of anything," I finish lamely.

"You mean like skydiving?" Clarice asks. She's still looking at her toes. She reaches down and runs her finger over her polish. "Why did y'all let me buy drugstore nail polish? It always flakes."

"No, not skydiving," I say. "Not like physical fear, more like, you know, emotional fear."

"Like going to a club and asking hot guys to dance," Marissa says, getting it.

"Why would you be afraid of that?" Clarice asks. Her face crumples up in confusion, and she slides her legs out from under her. "That's what you put in your notebook? That you're afraid to ask some guys to dance?" She looks at me skeptically, like I've just announced I'm afraid to go to school or something. Which, actually, now that I think about it, isn't that weird of a thing to be afraid of.

"Not, like, terrified of it," I say defensively. Which is sort of a lie. I might not be terrified, but I'm definitely scared. *Terrified* means "I think I'm going to die" or something. And I don't. At least, I don't think I do. Do I think I'm going to die if I ask guys to dance? Am I crazy? Like, even crazier than I first thought? Ohmigod. I'm totally going to have to go on meds! Just like Brian Abbott, who fell asleep right in the middle of lunch and drooled on the cafeteria table because he was on Xanax! Of course, I don't think it was prescription, but still.

"That's completely normal," Marissa says, nodding, and I relax a little. "To be nervous about that." She looks at Clarice over the table. "I'd like to see you do it."

Clarice shrugs and then pops up out of her chair. She smoothes her shirt down over her boobs, then takes a step toward the corner where the guy I'm supposed to be asking to dance is sitting.

"Noo!!" I almost scream, grabbing her arm. "You can't ask that one to dance, I'm supposed to do it."

"Fine," she says, shrugging her tiny shoulders. "I'll find someone else." And then she disappears into the crowd, where I watch her make her way over to the opposite corner, ask some random guy to dance, and then lead him onto the dance floor. There's hardly anyone else even dancing! Although it is getting a little busier in here. More and more people are streaming through the door, girls dressed in short skirts and dresses, guys in jeans and T-shirts. How come guys are allowed to wear jeans and T-shirts and girls have to wear heels and tight stuff? Of course, the more important question is why did I allow myself to be bossed into wearing heels and revealing stuff? It's so not me. I sigh and try to pull the top of my shirt up a little.

"Wow," Marissa says as she watches Clarice wrap her arms around the guy's neck. "I guess she wasn't kidding when she said she wasn't afraid."

"I guess not," I say morosely. Although if I looked like her, I wouldn't be afraid either.

"Wait until that guy she's dancing with finds out he's not getting any," Marissa says. "He's going to be so pissed." She keeps throwing glances over to the other side of the room, where Jeremiah is deep in conversation with Julia.

My cell phone vibrates in my pocket, and I pull it out. One new text. Cooper. "'TIME'S RUNNING OUT,'" it says. Time's running out? What does that even *mean*? No one said anything about there being a time limit on all of this. I mean, what does he think this is, an episode of *24*? I should be able to take my time. I look over to the corner, and Cooper's still there with a bunch of his dumb friends, calmly drinking his drink and laughing with them and not even looking at me.

"What does the text say?" Marissa asks. She gets in close to me and reads it. "'Time's running out'?" She frowns. "What does that mean?"

"It means," I say, "that if I don't do what they say, like, now, they're going to post my notebook online." Okay. I take a deep breath. I can do this. What's one second of humiliation compared to a lifetime of humiliation? Because, let's face it, that's what will happen if that notebook gets out. Much better to be laughed at by a random guy I don't know than have the whole school knowing my secrets.

"Uh-oh," Marissa says.

"What?" I ask. I look out onto the dance floor, which is rapidly becoming filled with people. Clarice is still dancing with the hottie, only now her back is to his front, and he's got his hands on her hips. Wow. I never knew Clarice had such good rhythm. She's like a little minx out there.

"Not Clarice," Marissa says, elbowing me. "Look."

I follow her gaze across the room until my eyes land on the guy I'm supposed to be asking to dance. Before, he was just sitting there all by himself, bopping his head to the music in this semi-dorky fashion. Now he is flanked by a girl on either side! And he is talking to them.

Well, not to both of them. One of the girls is talking to his friend. What? Where did his friend come from? He was by himself just two seconds ago. Now I'm going to have to ask him to dance in front of his friend! And two girls, both of whom have very, very long blond hair and are very, very tan. In November. Hello, girls, skin cancer, ever heard of it?

"You better go," Marissa says. "If he starts dancing with one of them . . ." She trails off, and I'm not sure if she means I'll never get a chance to ask him, or if he just won't want to dance with me. I don't stick around to find out, and before I can stop myself, I'm pushing through the crowd on my way over to the guy.

It becomes rather obvious rather quickly that even if I *did* want to ask this guy to dance, it's going to be, uh, kind of difficult. Their whole group is sitting in a round booth, and him and his friend are in the middle, with the two girls on the outside, surrounding them like some kind of security guards.

The weird thing is, I totally think they planned it. The girls, I mean. They planned it so that no one else could get at the guys. Unless those guys are their boyfriends. But that would be a complete disaster, so I decide to push that thought right out of my mind.

I stand by the side of the booth for a second, trying to come up with some sort of brilliant plan, but not sure exactly what to do. I mean, I've never done this before. And also, you know, it's awkward. Clarice made it look easy, yeah, but she didn't have to contend with OTHER GIRLS. I'm about to say forget it and just take the chance that my notebook is going to get passed around the school (humiliation that takes place in the future might be better than real, right-now, immediate humiliation) when I catch Cooper's eye across the room, and even though he's kind of far away and it's totally possible that I might be imagining it, I swear to God I see him smirk.

He smirks! At me! Well, more at the situation, like he doesn't think I can do it.

And so, before I can stop myself, I turn around and take a few steps until I'm standing in front of the table where my target is sitting.

"Hello," I say, plastering a huge smile on my face. But the music is pretty loud, and so they don't hear me. Either that, or they're just ignoring me. Which is a very real possibility. "Hello!" I say again, louder this time. One of the girls looks up at me.

"Hi," she says. She looks me up and down, then rolls her eyes and goes back to talking to the guy I'm supposed to be asking to dance. Okaaaay.

"Hey!" I try again, pretty much screaming now.

"Yeah?" the girl says. What is her problem? Doesn't she know that it is extremely obvious that I am not talking to her? Actually, now that I think about it, maybe it isn't.

"Not you," I say, forcing my smile to grow even bigger. Might as well be friendly. Don't want to start any weird competition thing, since, you know, it probably won't work out in my favor. The girl looks me up and down again, frowns, and then goes back to sipping her drink.

I look over my shoulder to where Marissa was sitting, but there are so many people here now that I can't see through the crowd. I'm about to scream again, when the guy I'm supposed to be asking to dance finally notices me standing there. He breaks out into a big smile, and my heart leaps up into my chest. He's smiling! Does that mean maybe he thinks I'm cute? I try to very covertly yank my shirt down a little to show some more cleavage.

"Hi," he says. I can't hear his voice that well over the music, but I think it might sound sexy. I swallow hard.

"Hi," I say. He's still smiling, and I start to feel a little more optimistic. He wouldn't be smiling if he thought I was completely gross, would he? Take that, blond suntan girls! And take that, 318s! This is going to be easier than I thought! Maybe he'll even become my boyfriend. Wouldn't that be awesome? Meeting the love of my life when I'm on this crazy —

"We'll have another round," he says, motioning to the table.

"Another what?" I ask, frowning. And then I get it. Oh. My. God. He thinks I'm a waitress! He is ordering drinks from me, like I am some kind of paid employee of THE CLUB, when I am supposed to be asking him TO DANCE.

"Another round," he says, slowly this time. Now he's looking at me like I might be slow.

"I'm not a waitress," I say. "Um, I came over here to ask you to dance."

The girl sitting with him snorts, like she can't believe how dumb that is. Her friend giggles, and *his* friend has the wherewithal to look embarrassed and study the bottom of his glass, where all that's left is some melted ice.

But to my surprise, the guy shrugs and then says, "Sure." Before I even realize what's going on, he's moving Blond Suntan Girl Number One over and getting out of the booth.

And then he's standing, taking my hand, and leading me through the crowd, right past Cooper Marriatti and onto the dance floor.

So, the thing is, I don't really know how to dance. Like, my experience with dancing is kind of . . . limited. And when I say *limited*, I mean, you know, nonexistent.

"My name's Rich," the guy says as he leans into me.

"I'm Eliza," I say back. But he doesn't seem to really hear. Or even care.

He reaches out and grabs my hips and before I know it, he's grinding on me. Like, really grinding on me. Yikes. Uh, it feels like he might be . . . um, pretty happy to be dancing with me, if you know what I mean. Which just goes to show that you cannot judge a person by how they look. This guy seemed like he was totally hot and completely unapproachable, but he's obviously easily excited and a little crazy.

"Thanks for saving me," he says. My arms are wrapped around his neck, and his lips are right against my ear. "That girl over there, the one who was sitting next to me? I slept with her last week and she totally won't leave me alone." He says it like wanting to hang out with someone that you slept with last week is the craziest thing he's ever heard.

"Oh," I offer brilliantly, because I'm not exactly sure how to respond to that. "That sucks."

"I met her here," he says. "I brought her home, and I should have known that she would show up here." He shakes his head sadly, like he can't believe his own stupidity.

He twirls me around, and as he does it, I catch Cooper's eye across the room, where he's sitting at the bar with the 318s. He has a shocked look on his face. Good. I hope he *is* shocked. I hope he realizes how completely and totally desirable I am. I hope he realizes what a huge mistake he made when he broke up with me. Not that I want him back or anything. No way. I would never go back to that lying, good-for-nothing, disgusting jerk. I wouldn't even talk to him, much less date him.

I pull Rich closer to me, realizing that Cooper has no idea

that he's only dancing with me so that he can avoid his stalker.

"You have nice big hips," Rich says.

"Thanks," I say, deciding to take it as a compliment. I close my eyes then and lose myself in the music. After a couple of songs, Rich leans into me and says, "That was fun, thanks." And then he's gone.

Well. Okay, then. I watch as he cuts through the crowd and heads to the other side of the club, where his friend is now waiting at a different table. I guess they've successfully ditched the Blond Suntan Girls. I almost feel sorry for them. The girls, I mean.

I head back to where Marissa and I were just sitting, but when I get there, she's gone. Three girls are sitting at our table now, and they don't seem too friendly. I look onto the dance floor to see if I can find Clarice, but she's not there either. And when I look back to the bar, the 318s seem to be gone too. I sigh, then push my way through the crowd and outside, to see if I can find my friends.

Chapter Four

8:37 p.m.

The air outside is cool and feels nice on my face after the damp, hot air of the club. But one glance around tells me no one's out here, either, so I walk a few steps outside to the side of the building to try and call Marissa, and when I do, I almost bump into Cooper.

"Oh," I say, pushing my hair out of my face. "Excuse me." I try to push by him but he doesn't seem like he wants to let me. I know this because he doesn't move. "Move," I say.

"Wait," he says. He looks around nervously, then glances behind him, like he's afraid he might be tailed by an assassin or something. Which is completely ridiculous. Honestly, they're really taking this whole secrecy thing just a little bit too far.

"What?" I ask. "You know, you're really taking this whole

thing a little too—" And then Cooper grabs my arm and pulls me over to the side of the building, before I can protest.

"Hey!" I say. "What are you doing? Let go of me!"

"Look," he says, releasing my arm when we're safely out of sight. Of who, I don't know. I rub my arm and pretend it's all sore, even though it doesn't hurt at all. "I'm not supposed to be talking to you, so just calm down and—"

My cell phone starts vibrating then, and I reach down and pull it out of my pocket. One new text message. "PLEASE PROCEED TO THE SPOTTED FROG," it says. It's from a number I don't recognize.

"Who is this from?" I demand, shoving the phone into Cooper's face.

"Um, Tyler," Cooper says. He's still looking around, all nervous and squirrelly-like.

"Right," I say. "Why does he want me to go to the Spotted Frog?" The Spotted Frog is a coffee shop around the corner from Cure. Marissa and I have gone there a couple of times, when we felt like going into the city and having brunch, or when we needed to cram for a test and wanted somewhere fun to study.

"He probably wants you to do something else from your notebook," Cooper offers up helpfully.

"Duh," I say, rolling my eyes. "When is he going to give it back?"

"I don't know," he says. "But listen, I'm going to help you. We can—"

"Where is it?" I demand.

"Where's what?" he asks.

"The notebook!" I say. Honestly!

"I don't know," he says. But his eyes shift to the right, which everyone knows is, like, the universal sign of lying, but it doesn't even matter because I don't need to know that sign since I already know he's a big liar.

"Excuse me," I say. I push past him and start to head back toward the front of the club. Cooper, proving just how ridiculous and stupid he is, follows me.

"Where are you going?" he asks. I'm walking super-fast, but Cooper, unfortunately, is having no trouble keeping up with me. It's these damn shoes I'm wearing. Whoever thought five-inch wedges were a good idea is obviously insane.

"I have to find Clarice and Marissa," I say.

"They're gone," he says.

"No, they're not," I say. Shows how much he knows. Clarice and Marissa would not just leave me. They know I'm in a state of duress.

"Yes, they are." I push past him, so not in the mood to deal with his craziness. But after another look around the club and calls to their cells that go unanswered, I realize he's right. They're gone. Clarice and Marissa are gone. They've deserted me.

Okay. New plan. Head to the Spotted Frog, where hopefully Tyler and the 318s are waiting to give me my notebook back after I do whatever ridiculous thing they have lined up for me next. Then, I will order a nice coffee or cappuccino and a chocolate-chunk cookie, and I will wait for Marissa and Clarice to call me, and then this whole night will be over, and we will all go back to my house and order romantic comedies off On Demand.

I go back outside, and Cooper is still standing there, leaning against the building.

I don't say anything and just start walking in the direction of the Spotted Frog. My phone starts vibrating in my pocket. Clarice. Thank God.

"*Where,*" I say, "the hell are you?"

"Oh." She sounds startled. "Sorry, I just . . . I thought you left."

"You thought I *left*?" Is she crazy? Why would she possibly think that I left? That makes no sense. Why would I leave? Where would I go?

"Yeah, Cooper told me you left." Oh. My. God. I'm going to kill him. I sigh and try not to explode from stress and frustration.

I also start to pick up my pace (well, as much as I can in these shoes), because as I walk down the street, I'm starting to realize that it's pretty dark out. And a little bit . . . rowdier, I guess you could say. Not that anything bad is happening. It's just that there are a lot more people on the street. And some of them are drunk already. At least, I think they're drunk. Either that, or they're just crazy. For example, a man wearing what looks to be a jacket made out of garbage bags just went by me, singing a Jackson 5 song at the top of his lungs.

"Look, where are you?" I ask Clarice.

"I'm in the VIP," she says. And then she adds, "With Derrick," like I should obviously know who Derrick is.

"Oh, that's nice," I say. "Who the hell is Derrick?" I cross the street over to the Spotted Frog, and stop outside the door, under the overhang. Cooper stops too, a few feet away from me. I glare at him, but he ignores me and just sits down at one of the tables outside and watches the people pass by. I look up and down the streets for a policeman. If I see one, I'm totally going to get a restraining order against Cooper. Although. I'm not sure you can get restraining orders just, you know, on the spot like that. But I can definitely get the policeman to tell him to leave me alone, and he can probably give me a restraining order form or something for me to fill out later.

"Derrick is the guy I was dancing with," Clarice says. "He totally got me into the VIP room, and he invited me over to his place after this."

"You're going to his *house*?" Is she crazy? Everyone knows you never, ever go to some strange guy's house. You inevitably end up maimed, murdered, or raped. At the very least, you end up drunk and making a sex tape that you totally regret once the guy leaks it on his blog.

"Not his house," she says, and I relax. "His apartment." Oh, Jesus. In the background, I can hear talking and laughing and the sound of voices and music.

"Um, Clarice? Don't you think that's a little dangerous?" I ask delicately. I know Clarice is from the South and all, and she gets totally shocked when people actually (gasp) lock their car doors, but this is taking it a little too far.

"No," she says. "I mean, it's not like I'm going alone. Butch and Kim are going to be there too."

"Who are Butch and Kim?" I ask.

"Derrick's friends," she says, sighing. Oh. Right. I guess that does help a little, since I don't think it would take three people to kill Clarice if that was Derrick's plan. She's pretty small. Of course, they could be some kind of murdering cult. And they could definitely try to convince her to be in a four-some sex video. "Do you want me to leave the VIP and come back down?" she asks.

I'm about to tell her yes, that I really want her to come and meet me, but then someone tugs on the back of my hair, and I turn around. Cooper. He is now standing right behind me, crowding my space.

"No," I say, anger rising up inside of me. "I got it." I flip my phone shut and whirl around. "What are you doing here?" I ask. Cooper looks taken aback.

"Following you," he says. "Obviously."

"Well, yeah," I say. "I mean, *why* did you follow me?"

"Because I'm supposed to be tailing you and making sure that you do everything we tell you."

"Why?" I narrow my eyes and hope I look menacing. Of course, it's very hard to look menacing when I'm completely scared shitless. And when college kids keep walking between us on their way into the Spotted Frog.

"Look," Cooper says. He moves closer to me so that people can get by. Which means he's very, very close. Closer than he's been since our breakup. I take a deep breath and try to stop myself from freaking out. "I want to help you."

"You want to help me? Have you completely and totally lost it?"

"Eliza, I know you're mad, but you don't get it. I didn't want to ever hurt you; I'm going to help you. They don't — "

"Oh, I get it all right," I say.

I push past him and into the Spotted Frog, then march over to a little table in the corner and sit down. The Frog's one of those places that's frequented by hipsters, mostly college kids who have turned their backs on the bar scene in favor of sipping organic teas and planting vegetable gardens and working on reducing their carbon footprints. The drinks are completely overpriced, and the people who work there can be a little annoying, with their whole "I'm so over you and everything else" attitudes, but somehow the vibe in there is warm and inviting.

Well. At least it is when you're there of your own accord and not because some psycho, dumb, secret, macho club at your school has basically blackmailed you into going there.

Cooper walks in behind me, and so I quickly take the extra chair at my table and shove it under the table next to me, where a girl with braids is sipping a chai tea and talking to her friend about her yoga class.

Cooper walks over and calmly removes the chair, puts it back at my table, and then sits down. Ugh. How annoying.

I pull out my phone and text Marissa. "WHERE. ARE. YOU??"

Cooper gets up and disappears for a second, then returns with two coffees.

"I got yours with cinnamon hazelnut syrup," he says.

I shoot him a glare, but take a sip of the warm liquid. It's so hot I almost burn my tongue, but it's good going down, comforting and sweet. "I'm not sure what I should thank you for first," I say. "Remembering how I take my coffee or turning me in to the dean because of what I wrote about you on Lanesboro Losers." I think that's a super-biting and witty remark that should totally put him in his place, but Cooper seems unfazed.

"I didn't turn you in," Cooper says. "That was the 318s." As he takes a sip of his coffee, one shirtsleeve slips down and I can see he's wearing the watch I bought him. Seriously! That is so screwed up. He should have to give me back all the presents I gave him while we were together.

"Give that back to me," I say, holding my hand out.

"Give what back to you?" Cooper asks. He sets his coffee cup down on the table.

"The watch I gave you."

"This?" Cooper holds up his wrist.

"Is that the watch I gave you?"

"Yes."

"Then yes."

"No," he says. "I love this watch."

"When people break up," I say, "they give back each other's stuff."

"This isn't each other's stuff," he says. "This was a gift."

"A gift given under false pretenses." I hold my hand out. "Give it back."

"No," he says. "I don't want to. The person who gets dumped gets to keep the gifts that were given to him."

"I didn't dump you," I say.

"Yes, you did," he says. "You left me that night."

"After I found a list that basically showed you were dating me as a joke? Yes, of course I left."

"That wasn't my list," he says. "It was the 318s' list."

"Isn't that kind of one and the same?" I ask. "Like, aren't you guys all supposed to be together, you know, brotherhood and one for all and all of that?" I roll my eyes so he can see just how stupid and ridiculous I think the whole thing is.

"I guess," he says. He pushes his cup back and forth between his fingers, sliding it on the table. Then he looks up at me, and he's looking right at me, and it's too intense and so I look away.

"Whatever," I say. "You can keep the dumb watch." I look down at the table and hope he couldn't hear the catch in my voice because, suddenly, I feel like I want to cry.

"Thanks," he says quietly. And then he doesn't say anything else.

"So what now?" I ask, blinking back the tears and forcing myself to look at him. "Am I supposed to strip down and flash everyone here or something?" I rack my brain for what I would have written in my notebook about the Spotted Frog, but I'm coming up blank. I haven't been here enough for it to really deserve a place in my notebook.

"What did that guy say?" Cooper asks suddenly, ignoring my comment about the flashing. And about what I'm supposed to do next.

"What guy?" I ask, confused.

"The one you were dancing with at Cure."

"You mean like what did we talk about when we were dancing?"

"No," Cooper says. "What did he say when you asked him to dance?"

"Um, he said, 'Sure.'" Cooper looks taken aback. "You don't have to look so shocked, Cooper, not everyone judges people on how much skin they're showing or how good they look in a bikini."

"I don't judge people on those things."

"Is that why you're hooking up with Isabella Royce?"

"Isabella Royce?" Cooper sits up straight. "Who told you I was hooking up with Isabella Royce?"

But before I can answer him, one of the hipster, "I'm so totally over it" workers, a guy with five earrings in each ear, is up on the stage that covers half of the café in the back.

"Hello," he says into the microphone that's set up. He taps on it and then says, "Testing, one two three" and somehow he's able to make it seem totally ironic.

"We're going to get started," he says. "So please pick your song and sign up over there." He points over to the corner, where a middle-aged woman is setting up what looks like a karaoke folder.

"Great," I say. "Now not only do I have to sit here and wait for some kind of direction, but now I'm going to have to listen to crazy people sing karaoke." The weird thing is, I don't mind listening to karaoke. I mean, what's not to like? People making total asses of themselves? Fun! It's just so annoying that I have to do it now, here, with Cooper.

Plus the Spotted Frog does karaoke as part of their "performance" series, where they have a different kind of entertainment every night. Usually they do poetry readings or have little indie bands play music in the corner, but once a month they do karaoke. People pretty much sing only indie music or girl rock, and the Spotted Frog tries to pretend it's all retro. So not as fun as the normal kind of karaoke.

Then Cooper gets this look on his face, the same look Clarice and Marissa got earlier, one of those "how do I tell her this?" kind of looks.

"What?" I ask. "Why are you looking at me like that?"

"Um, you know you're supposed to do karaoke, right?"

My heart sinks as I realize one of the things I wrote about in my purple notebook is how I wish I could get up and sing karaoke. Shit, shit, shit. Why did I write that? Why, why, why? I have no aspirations to be a singer. At all. In fact, I'm a horrible singer. Which I guess is why I always thought it would be cool to sing karaoke. I mean, it takes a lot of self-confidence to get up and do something that you know you're not good at. And that's the thing about karaoke—it almost doesn't really matter how good a singer you are—people care more about how much you get into it. If you get up there and act like you're really excited and think you're a rock star, people love it.

"I am?" I croak out.

"Yeah," Cooper says.

"Here?" I look around at the crowd. This is definitely not the kind of place that loves hearing the latest Britney Spears song belted out at the top of someone's lungs. This place would scoff at such a thing. This place wants you to sing Ani DiFranco and Tori Amos and bands people have never, ever heard of and never will again once they leave here.

Right now, for example, two girls are over at the folder, pouring through the songs, and I totally just heard one of them say, "Ooh, Fiona Apple, that is so nineties perfect."

"So did you get his number?" Cooper's asking.

"Whose number?" I ask.

"The guy you were dancing with," he says.

"Rich?"

"Oh, you know his name now?" Cooper narrows his eyes and takes another sip of his coffee.

"Why wouldn't I know his name?" I ask.

"He just didn't seem like the kind of guy who would take the time to ask you your name, if you know what I mean."

"Cooper, we were dancing. Of course he asked me my name."

Cooper snorts again and takes another sip of his coffee.

"Not everyone," I say, "is a sex-crazed maniac." Not that Cooper's sex-crazed. Although I wouldn't necessarily say he *isn't* sex-crazed either. I'd put his sex-crazedness at a normal level. Of course, that could just be for me. His sex-crazedness level for Isabella Royce could be through the roof.

"I'm not a sex-crazed maniac." Cooper looks shocked and offended.

"No one said you were," I say, wrapping my hands around my cup of coffee and enjoying his obvious discomfort. "I was just saying that Rich isn't." Which isn't exactly true. Okay, it's not even close to true. Rich was sex-crazed enough to take a girl home from the club with him and then never call her again. Is this enough to make someone a maniac? I'm not sure. Either way, Cooper totally doesn't need to know about the girl at the club or the fact that Rich was dancing with me only to get away from her.

"You said, 'Not everyone is a sex-crazed maniac' which implies that I am," Cooper says. "Which I'm not."

"If you say so," I say, and shrug. "But it sounds to me like maybe you have a guilty conscience."

"I don't have a—" Cooper clears his throat and leans across the table. "Is this about that night in the pool?"

Oh. That night in the pool. I'd totally forgotten about that. One night, when Cooper's parents were out, he invited me over for dinner. We grilled hamburgers on the deck and ate them on paper plates, and then we went swimming and we started making out, and Cooper was totally pushing it, trying to get it past third-base territory, but I wouldn't let him.

"Why do you care anyway?" I say. "That's ancient history."

"I don't," he says. His phone starts vibrating, and he picks it up and checks his texts. "They want to know if you're karaokeing."

"Can't you . . ." I try to act like I don't care and avert my eyes. "Can't you just tell them that I am? That I did?"

"Eliza," he says. "I can't." I see pity in his eyes, which really, really pisses me off. Actually, I'm mostly mad at myself, for even suggesting to Cooper that he help me. So before I can stop myself, I'm getting up and walking over to the corner, where the woman is setting up the karaoke machine.

"Do you have any Britney Spears?" I ask.

Chapter Five

9:01 p.m.

This is horrible. This is beyond horrible. I mean, talk about rubbing salt in my wounds. Is it not enough that I've been dumped and left brokenhearted? Now I have to be completely humiliated as well? Just because I wrote something totally dumb on a ridiculous website?

The woman behind the karaoke table has a British accent and crazy curly gray hair, and she's looking at me nervously, like she can't figure me out. Which makes sense. I mean, everyone else in here is wearing hemp, and I'm wearing platform heels with studs on them. "I think I left all the Britney back at the office, love." She starts flipping through the binder that lists all the songs, like maybe some rogue Britney might have slipped in there somewhere. "Um, will Christina Aguilera do?" she asks hopefully.

"I guess so," I say glumly. But then I remember all those people who try out for *American Idol* and sing a Christina Aguilera song and end up booted, and everyone in the audience shakes their head sadly and thinks, "Oh my God, what a fool. Why would anyone choose Christina? That is such a mistake."

"Actually, uh, no," I say. "Do you have anything else?"

"I think I have an old Justin Timberlake song in here somewhere." She pulls out a disc and holds it up. "It's a compilation." She smiles at me proudly.

"Great," I say. I write my name down on the list and then turn my back on Cooper and sit down at a table in the corner. I never should have asked him if he would lie for me. I mean, yes, he *is* a liar, but his lying is obviously exclusive to me, and to think otherwise shows a certain level of insanity on my part.

I look around. I guess the good thing about this place is that no one's really paying attention to the Fiona Apple girls who are singing right now. They're all, you know, way too cool to be interested in karaoke. Even karaoke that is supposed to be ironic and hip.

Cooper crosses the room in three long strides and sits down next to me.

"Ugh," I say, turning my seat away from him. I pick up a magazine that someone left on the table and start flipping through the pages. "Stop following me."

"I have to," he says. "To make sure you're doing what you're supposed to."

"Just shut up," I say. "If you have to follow me around, fine, but don't talk to me." I don't want him to talk to me because obviously I hate him, but also because I don't trust myself around him. His closeness is making my stomach do flip-flops, and I really don't want to cry in front of him, or bring up our breakup, or . . . just, yeah. Being close to Cooper is not a good idea.

Cooper reaches into his pocket, pulls out his cell phone, and snaps a picture of me.

"What was *that* for?" I ask. I hold my hands up in front of my face like he's a paparazzi stalker, which really makes no sense, since, you know, he already took the picture.

"So I can show Tyler," he says. "They need to know you're here." He looks apologetic.

"They don't trust you enough to tell them the truth?" I ask, grinning. "They need photographic evidence?"

"I guess so." He looks like this just hit him. I grin some more.

"Thank you, Helena and Rose," the karaoke woman is saying. "And now, we have Eliza, performing "Sexy Back" by Justin Timberlake." A giggle ripples through the crowd. Hmmph. I guess they're not too cool to make fun of others. And they're definitely not too cool to scoff at Justin Timberlake. Damn. I really should have used a fake name.

"Eliza, dear, where are you?" she asks. She looks around and finally, I get up, walk to the front of the stage, and take the microphone from her. My hands are shaking, and she puts the Justin Timberlake DVD into the player, so that the words can flash across the screen for me to sing along with.

It's at that moment I realize this is a horrible plan. Yes, the whole thing is a horrible plan, doing what the 318s say and letting my notebook fall into the wrong hands, but the more horrible thing is that I HAVE PICKED A JUSTIN TIMBERLAKE SONG. "Sexy Back," no less!

I thought I was being coy, picking a song that no one would care about but, really, it's having the opposite effect. People are interested because they think it's so stupid. And when I think about it, it *is* a pretty stupid song. "I'm bringing sexy back"? What does that even mean? Not to mention that it's pretty arrogant. Like, bringing sexy back all by yourself? *Justin* even got crap for it, I think. Can you imagine what these people are going to think about ME singing that I'm bringing sexy back?

Ohmigod, ohmigod, ohmigod. My mouth starts to get all dry, and I really wish I had some water.

The music starts then, and suddenly it's like a movie, one of those really bad movies where the person is supposed to be in a talent show or auditioning for something or singing in front of people, and they just FREEZE. That is what is happening right now. I am just freezing.

The words are starting to move across the screen, but I can't open my mouth. Everyone in the whole place is staring at me, which is making it even worse, and I'm sure it's my imagination, but it seems like more people are coming in, like some kind of announcement got posted somewhere saying that some weird girl was singing Justin Timberlake in the hipster café and her name is Eliza and everyone should come watch.

I take a deep breath. Okay. There is nothing to this. It is just singing. In fact, I've sung this song tons of times. Of course, I was alone in my room at the time, using my hairbrush as a microphone and making up my own dance moves while pretending to be famous. But still. It's just karaoke, and I am never going to see any of these people again. I try and picture them all naked. Then I close my eyes and pretend I'm back in my room. But it's not working. Nothing is coming out of my mouth.

"Come on!" someone yells. I open my eyes. It's some jerk college guy who looks like maybe he's the type to put expensive whiskey in one of those silver flasks and then carry it around, thinking it makes him seem super-classy and not just like he's trying to get drunk in the middle of the day. "Show us how you're going to get sexy back!"

Then, suddenly, just when I think the crazy, drunk flask guy is going to get up and say something again, or maybe throw his flask at me the way people used to throw tomatoes, Cooper is out of his chair and standing next to me. He takes the microphone out of my hand and starts to sing. What? Why? Cooper is now standing next to me, singing "Sexy Back" by Justin Timberlake!

"What are you *doing*?" I whisper.

"Helping you," he whispers back. The thing about Cooper is that even though he's a jerk, he definitely has, you know, that something. That thing I was talking about that allows certain people to be good at karaoke. He's suddenly gyrating all over the place, totally getting into it, and acting like he really is bringing sexy back.

And to my surprise, people are actually starting to like it. Of course, I guess it isn't really that surprising. Cooper is very good-looking. And charming. Which is how he charmed me into losing my mind and going out with him. He's also not that bad of a singer, although his strength definitely lies in his performance. I'm so caught up in what he's doing, that when he puts the microphone in my face to sing backup, I chime right in and sing, my panicked feeling gone.

We do the whole song like that, him putting the microphone out once in a while and me screaming song lyrics into it. Finally, at the end of the song, Cooper leaves me up there to do the last bit, and then takes a pic of me on his cell phone, I guess to text to the 318s. And then, just like that, the music is over, and the nice British woman is taking the microphone from me. "Thanks," I say to Cooper. Because that was pretty nice of him. To save me like that, I mean.

And so for a second, I let myself believe that maybe Cooper was telling the truth, that maybe the 318s were the ones who took my notebook and turned me in to the dean, that maybe he doesn't even care about what I wrote on Lanesboro Losers, that maybe we can talk and I can find out *why* exactly he did what he did. I mean, he *is* wearing the watch I gave him after all. But Cooper just squeezes my shoulder, whispers, "You're welcome" into my ear, and then walks out of the Spotted Frog, leaving me there by myself.

Well, of course he did. Leave right when I thought we were having some kind of moment, I mean. First of all, Cooper is obviously completely and totally unstable. Look what he did to me, for example. Pretending that he liked me, just for some dumb secret society initiation? That is definitely the work of a sociopath. Actually, I'm not sure what a sociopath is, exactly. But I think it has to do with not caring about the feelings of others.

Anyway, the point is, something is definitely wrong with him. So it makes total and complete sense that he would help me one minute, then turn on his heel and walk out the next, acting all put out, like I asked him for help or something. He's so crazy, it's pathetic.

I walk out of the Spotted Frog and look around. It's after nine o'clock, but Boston is alive with people, walking around and looking happy, couples on their way to a late dinner in their nice clothes, college kids walking around drunk, groups of girls giggling on their way to bars and clubs. A homeless man on the side of the street looks me up and down and says, "Girrrl, you got it going on."

I give him a dollar and actually start to feel a little better. I mean, I just got a super-hot guy to dance with me at Cure, *and* I did karaoke. Not bad for a Saturday night. And yeah, okay, maybe it's not that amazing for *some* people but it's amazing for me. Who cares if Rich just wanted to avoid his stalker, and Cooper had to help me with the karaoke?

I start to feel very happy, until I realize I have no clue what I'm supposed to do next. I'm alone, in the city, with no idea where my friends are or when they're coming back. And then my phone rings. Marissa. Thank God.

"Hello?" I say.

"Hi," she says. "You gotta get over here."

"Um, over where?"

"That's right, honey," the homeless man near me says. "You look like a supermodel, for reals. Mmmm mmm." Hmm. I start to move away slowly.

"To Isabella Royce's apartment." The other thing about Isabella Royce? You know, besides the fact that she's hooking up with Cooper? She has her own apartment. Well, technically it's not hers. Yet.

See, Isabella's grandmother died a few months ago and left her this amazing apartment right on Newbury Street, which is like the nicest, most expensive street in Boston. Apparently it was this big debacle, since Isabella's mom totally thought the apartment was going to be left to her, but it turned out that Isabella's grandmother, like, secretly hated her mom. (This was her dad's mom, by the way. Isabella's dad passed away a while ago, which is why it was so important for her mom to get this apartment, since apparently it's worth like a billion dollars and Isabella's mom was going to sell it so that she would never have to work again.)

Anyway, the apartment got left to Isabella but put under the care of her uncle or something, until she turns eighteen next year. In the meantime, her uncle has it all fixed up and lets her use it anytime she wants.

"What's going on at Isabella's?" I ask, looking around nervously for Pervert Homeless Man. But he's now inched his way down the sidewalk and has turned his attention to two college girls coming out of the Spotted Frog. Figures. Typical man, moving on to the next thing.

"She's having a party," she says. "And Jeremiah is going to be there."

"How do you know that?" I say. "And where are you?"

"I know," she says. "Because I, um, followed him. And I'm here. Outside of Isabella's."

"You followed who?" I ask.

"Jeremiah. And Julia. Out of Cure. But they didn't hook up or anything, I swear. In fact, he didn't even touch her. I watched them during their whole T ride. And now they're at Isabella's party. And I'm going in now, but I have to at least act like I'm meeting someone here, so you have to come."

"That's why I couldn't find you?" I ask. "Because you were *following Jeremiah*?" I try to keep my voice down, but I'm pissed.

"Eliza, I'm so sorry!" she says. "It just happened, I swear. I didn't mean to, I was just going to follow them a little way down the street, and then the next thing I knew, I was on the T!"

"Why didn't you at least text me?" I ask.

"You know the service on the T is super-spotty," she says. I think about yelling at her for ditching me, but then decide it's not really worth it. I mean, I have way bigger problems right now. "So will you come?" she asks. "To Isabella's?"

"Fine," I say, starting to feel very cranky. Isabella Royce's party is the last place I want to be. Also, who knows what Cooper and the 318s have in store for me next. But what else am I supposed to do? I sigh and end the call, then slide my phone into my bag and head to the nearest T.

When I get down to the T, I realize my subway card is out of money. My subway card is always out of money, which makes no sense, since I hardly ever ride the T, and every time I do, I always make sure to put at least three rides on my card.

I add ten dollars to it using the automatic machine, then double-check my phone, just in case Cooper or the 318s have sent me another text. But they haven't, so I shove my card into my pocket and head down to the platform.

Everything's fine for the first couple of minutes, but then it happens. I hear the voice. The very loud, very shrieky, very familiar voice. Isabella Royce.

"OH MY GOD, ELIZA! WHAT ARE YOU DOING HERE?" She takes me by the hands and pulls me close to her, giving me a kiss on each side of my face. Sigh. Of all the people to be down here, Isabella Royce is the worst. It's not that I don't like Isabella, per se. It's just that seeing her reminds me of Cooper. And besides, shouldn't she be at her own party?

"Just, you know, riding the T!" I say brightly. What else would I be doing down here?

"I know that," she says, giggling. "I mean, where are you going?"

Oh. Right. "Um, actually, to your apartment," I say. Then I realize that I wasn't even technically invited to Isabella's apartment, that Marissa stalked Jeremiah there and then invited herself and me.

But Isabella doesn't seem to mind. "Me too!" she exclaims. "What a coincidence!"

"Not really," I say, even though it kind of is.

"Well yes, really," she says, as the train pulls up. It's loud, so I can't hear exactly what she's saying, but I think it has something to do with how she can't believe that we'd both be at this T stop at this exact time, because usually she just drives in, but she was returning some shoes and ohmigod now we can keep each other company. I don't ask her why she was returning shoes so late at night, since (a) I don't really care and (b) I'm not sure if I even heard her right.

So I just smile and nod.

"So," she says once we're settled on the train. The train is actually pretty dead, and so we unfortunately have no problem finding seats next to each other. "Are you going to the party alone, or . . . ?" She trails off and then gets super-busy looking through one of the shopping bags she has with her, and I can tell she's trying to sound innocent. I decide to make an effort to try to be nice to Isabella. After all, what Cooper did isn't her fault.

"Um, no," I say. "I'm meeting Marissa there."

"Oh, cool," she says, and I see her face relax. Like, I literally see it relax. It just sort of . . . deflates. And then I realize why. She was afraid that maybe I was going to the party because I knew Cooper would be there! Am I a pity case? Does Isabella Royce think I'm a loser? Is she maybe afraid that if I don't get a new boyfriend, I'm going to maybe go psycho on her and freak out and key her car or something? Isabella DOES have a very nice car, this totally cute red convertible that's not brand-new enough to be pretentious, but not old enough to be lame.

I decide it's time to change the subject.

"So you know people are already there, right?" I ask. "At your apartment, I mean."

"Um . . ." she looks down at the ground and messes around with the bottom of the skirt she's wearing. "Yeah, actually. Cooper's watching it for me."

"Oh," I say. "Cool." So that explains why he rushed out of the Spotted Frog so fast. He had a date to watch Isabella's party. Like they're married or something! He probably has a key and everything. Not only that, but I am now inadvertently following the person that I want to get away from and am going to have to see him and Isabella together, and he might think that I followed him there on purpose. Ugh, ugh, ugh. I make a mental note to kill Marissa.

"Yeah," Isabella says. "I know you guys had a bad breakup and everything, but honestly things have been super-good with us ever since we've been hanging out." That's probably because their relationship is based on their, you know, actually *having* a relationship and not some dumb prank.

"That's great," I say, forcing myself to at least try and sound happy. Across the aisle, a man with a beard and cargo pants is ogling Isabella's legs. She's wearing a very short, glittery lavender skirt and gold platform shoes. What is up with everyone dressing like this in November? I guess on Saturday nights in the city sexiness trumps comfort.

"How's Kate liking college?" Isabella asks, oblivious to the attention she's getting.

"Um, she's liking it," I say. Which is true.

"That's so great," she says. "I can't even *begin* to think about going to college, I mean, it's going to be so crazy, it's like . . ." Isabella starts chattering on and on, but I'm kind of tuning her out because I can't stop thinking about her and Cooper. Does he love her? Has he *told* her he loves her? Are they going to get married? Have they had sex? My head is spinning with all these crazy thoughts, and so at first I don't realize Isabella's stopped talking and is now looking at me expectantly.

"Totally," I say. "College is going to be crazy. I'm really glad we're not seniors this year." This is a lie, since suddenly I really want nothing more than to be out of this school and away from all these people, but something tells me Isabella wouldn't really appreciate this sentiment.

"Totally," she says, her eyes wide. She gets a very serious look on her face. "I just don't understand those people who want to get out of here. It's like, hello! Your classmates are the people you've grown up with, they're part of your history!"

"Exactly," I say, pretending I agree with her. The train stops, and Isabella hops right out of our car I pretend to be looking for something in my purse, hoping that maybe she'll get lost in the crowd on the platform. But when I leave the train, Isabella's there, waiting for me and smiling.

"Ready?" she asks.

"Ready," I say. And then I follow her up the stairs and onto the street.

When we get to the party, Isabella waves and says, "See ya!" then disappears into the crowd of people in her living room. I'm insulted for a second, but then realize I can't totally blame her. I mean, Isabella and I aren't *really* friends. Unfortunately, I have only one friend here, and I don't see her anywhere. In fact, the only people I see here are all of Isabella's friends.

"Oh," Jessica Adams says when she sees me. "Is Kate here?" She looks past me toward the door, as if the only reason I'd dare to show up at this party would be because my sister was with me.

"Uh, no," I say. "She's not."

"Oh." Jessica looks disappointed (a visit from Kate, a super-popular college girl who still gets talked about at our school even though she graduated last year, would make this party the talk of the school on Monday), but she recovers quickly. "Well, there's drinks in the kitchen." She disappears down the stairs.

I pull my phone out and call Marissa. "Where. Are. You?" I ask when she answers. I can tell she's here, because the sounds coming through the other end of my cell phone are the same things I can hear, namely people talking and music coming through an iPod that's hooked up to the ginormous stereo system.

"Over in the corner, with Delia Carhart," she says. I look over, spot them, and make my way through the crowd. No sign of Cooper or the 318s.

"Did you get it back?" Marissa asks when she sees me.

"No," I say. "Although I did sing karaoke at the Spotted Frog." I'm about to add, "with Cooper" but then realize that (a) I shouldn't be talking about him since I don't care if I did something with him, karaoke or otherwise, and (b) with Delia standing right here, it's probably not a good idea to talk about it.

"I love that place, the Spotted Fraaahg," Delia says, drawing the word out. "They have the best mocha lattes."

"Yeah," I say. Now that I think about it, I don't like Delia that much. One time we had to be partners in history and she made me do the whole project by myself.

"That place is really fun," Marissa says. Then she throws her head back and laughs, which is kind of weird, since it's not that funny. But then I spot Jeremiah over in the corner, and I get it. She's trying to act like we're having such a great time

74

over here that she's not even noticing that he's there. Which is the oldest trick in the book, and so he can probably see right through it. Although maybe not. I don't think Jeremiah Fisher is that bright. One time I had to explain to him what irony was, and he still didn't get it.

"Anyway," I say, "Marissa, come with me to get a drink."

Delia gets the message and puts a pissed, put out sort of look on her face, but then turns around and goes off to bother someone else.

We head into the kitchen, where Marissa drinks a soda, and I look around for something a little stronger. I'm not that great with alcohol, and since I've already had a few sips of a cosmo, I need to be careful. I tend to get drunk very fast, probably because I don't really drink that often. I spot a pitcher of something pink sitting on the counter next to a stack of plastic cups. Not just any plastic cups, though. They're plastic cups with purple-and-aqua decals all over them. Of course Isabella would have cups like that.

I pour some of the pink liquid into the purple-and-aqua cup and hope that no one's spiked it with a date-rape drug.

"So," Marissa says. "Was he, you know, watching me?"

"Who?" I ask, frowning. I take a sip of the pink drink. Very strong, but very good, sweet and tangy. I take another sip. A small one.

"Jeremiah!" Marissa says. "Duh!" I notice she's taken her sweater off and is now wearing just a light yellow halter top. Also, her shoulders look very sparkly.

"What's all over your shoulders?" I ask, moving in for a closer look.

"Body sparkles," she says. "I took them out of Isabella's room."

"Isabella already has a room here?" I ask.

"Yeah, totally," she says. "With all her makeup, a fully stocked closet, everything."

"That is so cool," I say. Wow. I mean, how fun! To have your own apartment with, like, duplicates of all your stuff. Think about it. You could just come into the city to hang out anytime you want. I wonder just how popular Isabella would be if she didn't have this apartment. Hmm. Probably still really popular, since she's gorgeous.

"So was he?" Marissa asks.

"Was who what?" I take another sip of my drink, a bigger one this time. I'm starting to feel a little bit warm inside, and it feels good, but I know enough to realize that there's a fine line between feeling all warm and good inside and ending up puking into the bushes while people shake their head sadly at you and mumble things about how you can't hold your liquor. Not that that's happened to me before. But I do know some people it *has* happened to, cough, Jeremiah, cough.

"Was. Jeremiah. Watching. Me." She takes the cup I'm holding out of my hand and pours its contents down the sink.

"Hey!" I say. "What'd you do that for?" I watch sadly as the pink liquid goes pouring down the drain, circling around and then disappearing forever.

"Because you're having problems paying attention to the conversation already," she says.

"No, I'm not," I say, shocked.

She looks at me and raises her eyebrows.

"Okay, well, maybe I am, but that's just because I'm a little bit distracted," I say. "Not because I'm getting drunk." It's totally true, too. I'm distracted by the fact that my life is about to be over, not because of the alcohol. "I only had two sips," I point out.

She hands me a soda, and at the same time, I feel my phone vibrating in my bag.

"Oh, God," I say, feeling nervous. I pull my cell out and look at the screen. One new text. From Tyler. "ATTEMPT TO MAKE OUT WITH NIGEL RICKSON."

"Oh. My. God," I say.

"What is it?" Marissa asks. "Is it from Cooper?"

"No," I say. "It's from Tyler." I show her the screen.

"Oh my God," she says.

"I know!" Okay, deep breaths. I will NOT freak out. Marissa doesn't say anything, just pours me another pink drink into a plastic cup. I take a sip, but it's totally lost its luster. Also now I have to be afraid of possibly maybe puking all over Nigel Rickson if I try to kiss him and am too drunk.

"Why would they . . ." Marissa starts, frowning. "I mean, how did they . . . ?"

"I wrote it down," I say. "In my notebook."

"Right," Marissa says. She looks at the floor.

Here's the deal with Nigel Rickson: I used to be in love with him. And when I say, *in love with him,* I (obviously) mean from afar. He's from England and he showed up at our school freshman year with this totally sexy British accent. He was into all this weird hip-hop music and he wore baggy clothes and had braces which totally somehow worked on him and made him seem very badass. Like how some rappers have gold teeth?

Anyway, the braces are long gone, but the hip-hop clothes are still there, and Nigel Rickson and his friends still walk down the hallways at school listening to underground hip-hop on their iPods and spend their weekends scouting artists for the record label Nigel is going to start one day.

My crush on Nigel was one of those crushes that at the time was super-strong, until one day I had Clarice ask Nigel what he thought of me, and he seemed kind of clueless as to who I was, and it made me really upset and I spent all of the next week obsessing over him and listening to sad love songs in my room.

And after that, I was pretty much over him. Although sometimes when we're in a class together I'll find myself staring at him and sort of daydreaming about what it would be like to make out with him. Also, one time I kind of saw that he has a little bit of hair on his stomach, like this little trail that sort of goes from his belly button, um, down, and you'd think that would seem really gross, but it wasn't, it was super-sexy and made my head get all wobbly and I almost passed out in gym class. Of course, that could have been because we were running the mile that day, but I don't think so.

Anyway, up until Cooper, I guess you could say he was my longest crush. Like, of course I'd had crushes on guys after that and before that, but Nigel is the one who I've always kind of come back to. Until Cooper, and then I kind of forgot that Nigel existed.

Isn't that funny? Or maybe even ironic? I mean, now they want me to try to make out with Nigel, and it shouldn't even be that scary, because I don't like him anymore, but it still is pretty scary because it means I have to, you know, try to get him to kiss me.

"You'll be fine," Marissa says. Her voice sounds confident, but her face doesn't look so sure.

"Where is he?" I ask. "Have you seen him?"

"Yeah, he's in the corner, with some of his friends. They were playing craps or something on the floor."

"They were playing what?"

"Craps, you know?" She mimes throwing something. "Like with dice."

Oh. Great. Not only do I have to figure out a way to get him to make out with me, but now I have to compete with gambling? There's no way I'm going to win that battle.

"Give me your iPhone," I demand.

Marissa hands it over. I scroll through her apps until I find Pandora. If I'm going to do this, I at least need something to talk to him about. I'll find a good rap artist, listen to some songs, and use that as a conversation opener. But in my heightened state of despair, the only rap artists I can think of are mainstream rap artists. Which is fine, but I need something more impressive. Something that will make him think we have a connection, me and Nigel, two rap aficionados.

"What are some underground Boston rap artists' names?" I ask Marissa.

She looks at me. "Are you seriously asking me that?"

Hmmm. I rack my brain, trying to remember at least one person or group. I should be able to. I mean, when I was a freshman I totally spent a whole weekend scouring the internet for local Boston rap artists so that I could impress Nigel with my knowledge in study hall the next day. Of course, I chickened out and didn't talk to him, but still. Damn. What was that one guy's name? Mr. something. Or maybe it was a group? That's the other problem with underground rappers, you can never tell from their names if they're solo artists or groups.

"Mr. Rift!" I scream. "That's the name of that one guy, Mr. Rift!" I start plugging it into Marissa's phone.

"Mr. Rift," Marissa says thoughtfully. She takes another sip of her drink. "I like it. It sounds kind of . . . old school. But hip."

I don't ask her what she means by that, because I'm still looking for songs to listen to and because Cooper picks that moment to come waltzing into the kitchen like an asshole.

"Oh," he says, when he sees me and Marissa.

"Oh?" Marissa says, looking at him coolly. "Is that really all you have to say for yourself?" She crosses her arms, like maybe she might be ready to fight. Which is crazy. Marissa never fights. Well. Except for one time in seventh grade when Meredith Cosanti stole her sports bras and wouldn't admit it. But that was junior high, everyone was fighting in junior high.

"Marissa," I say, warning her. I'm plugging *Mr. Rift* into Pandora, but it's not coming up. "Is there any other way to spell *rift*?" I ask.

"*R-I-F-T*," Cooper recites. I ignore him and turn my back on him, speaking directly to Marissa.

"Is there?" I ask. "Any other way to spell it?"

"I don't think so." She frowns.

"Why do you need to spell *rift*?" Cooper asks. He walks over and looks over my shoulder at the screen of Marissa's iPhone. There's nowhere for me to go, since the counter is right behind me, and Cooper's arm brushes against mine, making my head feel all wobbly and fizzy. I tell myself it's the drinks, even though I only had three sips.

"None of your business," I say, pulling the phone out of his line of sight. But it's too late—he's already seen what I was trying to do.

"Do you mean . . . do you mean *Mr. Lif*?" he asks. "The rapper?"

"No," I lie, but I'm already plugging in the right name. Mr. Lif! I should have remembered, since I made up this (obviously not very effective) mnemonic device when I had to remember it the first time. Something to do with elevators, I think.

"Why are you looking up Mr. Lif?" Cooper asks. He's leaning over me again, trying to get a look at the iPhone. He smells like soap and shampoo and that same yummy smelling cologne. Wait a minute. I give the air another sniff.

"Are you . . . are you wearing the cologne I gave you?" I ask incredulously.

"No." He gets a panicked look on his face and takes a step back.

"Yes, you are," I say, narrowing my eyes. For some reason, this bothers me even more than the watch. I mean, I gave him that cologne as a present. Because I liked the smell of it and because I wanted to do something nice for him. Not so he could go around wearing it, probably so he can get Isabella all hot and bothered and have his way with her.

"Take it off," I demand. Which makes no sense, since how do you take off cologne? I mean, I guess you could wash it off, but is Cooper really going to do that? And he would have the whole rest of the bottle, anyway. Although from the way he smells, it doesn't seem like he'd have much left.

"I can't take it off," he says.

"Don't ever wear it again," I command.

He rolls his eyes. "You don't *own* the cologne."

I skip a few songs on Pandora until a Mr. Lif song comes on. Hmm. This is actually kind of catchy. You know, if you like that kind of thing.

"This is kind of catchy," Marissa says. "If you like that kind of thing."

Jeremiah Fisher peeks his head into the kitchen. He looks around, sees Marissa, and gives her a huge smile. "Hey," he says. "There you are!"

Oh my God. I mean, *seriously*. She's been here for at least thirty minutes, he must have seen her before this. And he's just now coming over to say hi to her. How lame. On the bright side, now my best friend and I are both in the same situation, i.e., having to tell stupid men where they can go and stick their stupid lines and games. Now Marissa and I can bond together in a show of sisterhood and feminism.

But of course, Marissa just smiles at him, flips her hair back, giggles, and says, "Yup, here I am."

I sigh.

"Come hang with me," Jeremiah commands. And then he disappears before Marissa can answer him.

"You're not," I say.

"Why not?" she asks, biting her lip.

"You know why not," I say.

"Wait, you guys hooked up?" Cooper asks. "You and Jeremiah?"

"What, like she's not good enough for Jeremiah or something?" I demand.

"No, I didn't say that," Cooper says. He opens the refrigerator and pulls out a Tupperware bowl, then heads over to the drawer in the corner and pulls out a fork. "I just didn't think he was your type, Marissa, that's all."

"Don't tell her what her type is," I say to Cooper. "You

don't even *know* her." Which is kind of true, but kind of not. When Cooper and I were dating, he did spend a lot of time with Clarice and Marissa, mostly because I was determined not to lose myself in the whole "I have a boyfriend" thing and forget about my friends. But obviously I didn't want to lose Cooper, either, so we all spent a lot of time together.

"Why isn't Jeremiah my type?" Marissa asks, looking at Cooper with interest.

"Not smart enough for you," Cooper says. He's now eating what looks like some kind of pasta out of the container. Probably his own food left over from last night, when he was here with Isabella. He probably made her dinner, and then they had sex in the bedroom. Either that or he feels comfortable enough with her to just eat her food. I swallow around the lump that keeps popping up in my throat.

"Jeremiah's smart," Marissa protests.

"Not really," Cooper says. "I mean, he's not dumb or anything, he's smart when it comes to school stuff. But he doesn't like to analyze things the way you do."

"True," Marissa says. She twirls a strand of hair around her finger and thinks about it. Unbelievable! I've been telling Marissa this for, like, weeks and Cooper says it to her once, and she's considering it.

"Don't talk to her," I say to Cooper. "In fact, what are you even doing here?"

"I'll be in the living room," Marissa says. Evidently Cooper's observation about Jeremiah wasn't enough to keep her from following him out there. This makes me happy for some reason, even though it shouldn't.

"So why are you listening to Mr. Lif?" Cooper asks.

"Like you don't know," I say.

"I don't."

"I have to kiss Nigel," I say. "And so I figured that would be a good way for us to bond."

"You have to kiss Nigel?" Cooper asks. *"Nigel Rickson?"* He sets his bowl down on the island in the kitchen. "That's what they told you to do?"

"Yeah," I say. "That's what they told me to do."

"But you like Nigel," he says.

"Duh," I say. "Which is the reason I wrote about him in my notebook, which is the reason they're making me kiss him." I don't correct him to say that I *used* to like Nigel. Let him think I still do. And anyway, maybe I do. Maybe Nigel is the new Cooper. Maybe we're going to get married and live happily ever after. Of course, I thought that might happen with that guy Rich from the club, but still.

My phone rings then. Clarice. I answer it.

"We're at Isabella Royce's house," I say. "Where are you?"

"Um, leaving Derrick's apartment," she says.

"Did you have fun?"

"Not really," she says, sighing. "Butch and his girlfriend left. And so then me and Derrick were just listening to some music, and he had his arm around me, and it was really nice. But then I started telling him about Georgia, you know, and how different it is here, and then he started acting all antsy, like he wanted me to get out of there."

This is a pattern that happens sometimes with Clarice. Well, most of the time, actually, not just some of the time. She'll meet some guy, get invited over to his place, and when it becomes clear that she doesn't want to hook up, he'll either kick her out or make her feel like he wants her to leave. Usually this comes after Clarice has given him tons of signals that she *does* want to hook up, like, you know, going over to his house late at night. She's kind of a tease, although she doesn't realize it.

"Sorry," I say.

"Not a big deal," she says, sounding breezy. Clarice doesn't ever stay down for long. "So listen," she says, her voice bright. "I have a really great idea."

"You do?" I ask warily. The last time Clarice had a really great idea, she ended up with a tattoo of a Japanese symbol on her back that she had to get removed when she realized it meant "visitors welcome." Kind of ironic, when you think about it. Plus now's not really the time for great ideas. I'm in the middle of a pretty big personal crisis.

"Yes," she says. "I got it when Derrick was talking about something he did last year, for his senior prank."

"Okay," I say again. Out of the corner of my eye, I see Cooper throw the empty Tupperware bowl into the sink, then reach into the pantry and pull down a box of cookies. He holds them out to me, offering me one. I glare at him and then turn my back.

"Well, apparently Derrick and his friends had this huge prank planned, but it didn't really work out, so they had to do an alternate prank that involved stealing this guy's pet pig and, like, you know, letting it loose."

"Didn't that happen in a movie?"

"Didn't what happen in a movie?" she asks.

"That someone stole a pig and let it loose?"

"*Varsity Blues*," Cooper pipes up helpfully from behind me.

"*Varsity Blues*," I tell Clarice, my back still turned on Cooper. Which doesn't help, because I can still feel him behind me, eating and, you know, watching me or something.

"I don't know," Clarice says. She sounds confused. "Why would he tell me he did something that happened in a movie?"

"Maybe they got the idea from the movie, and so they did it themselves," I say, mostly because I don't have the heart to tell her that he probably lied in an effort to impress her and get her clothes off. Behind me, Cooper guffaws. I turn around and smack him on the shoulder.

"That's probably it," Clarice says. She sounds relieved. "Probably they stole that idea from the movie."

"Totally," I say. Cooper rubs his shoulder and puffs his lip out, pretending to pout, even though there's no way that hurt him.

"Anyway," Clarice says. "So that's when I got the idea. You know, on how we can get you out of this."

"You want us to steal a pig?" I ask.

"No-o-o-o," she says, sounding like she thinks I'm completely stupid for not getting it. "I want us to steal your notebook back."

Oh. My. God. Of course! Clarice is brilliant! Why hadn't any of us thought of this before? If we can somehow get my notebook back, then this whole charade will just . . . end. Because if I have the notebook, they can't do anything to me! They'll have nothing to hold over my head! Of course, I don't know where the notebook is. But if I can somehow figure it out . . . My heart leaps, and for the first time all night, I start to feel a little bit hopeful.

"Interesting," I say to Clarice slowly, so that Cooper doesn't know what we're talking about.

"I think so," Clarice says, sounding pleased with herself. "Anyway, I'm getting on the T now, so I'll see you soon."

I end the call and take a deep breath. Okay. New plan. Get through this whole dumb kissing thing, then figure out how to get the notebook back. Easy, right?

"Clarice ended up back at some guy's apartment again?" Cooper laughs, then holds the cookies out again.

"I said, 'no thank you,'" I say haughtily, even though my stomach is rumbling. I will not take any food from him, thank you very much, and definitely not any of Isabella's food. "And don't talk about Clarice like you know her. In fact, please don't talk to me at all."

Cooper gets a serious expression on his face then and sets his cookie on the counter. "Eliza," he says. "Listen, you . . ." He takes a deep breath and starts again. "You don't have to do this."

"Don't have to do what?"

"You don't have to go out there and try to kiss Nigel."

"Yes, I do," I say. He's moving toward me now, so I take a step back and the kitchen counter pushes into my lower back. For a second I have a flashback of how it used to be, when Cooper and I were together. I'd be leaning against my locker before second period history, and he'd have his arms around my waist, trying to kiss me, and I'd be pushing him away because I was always afraid of getting into trouble, even though I totally wanted to kiss him.

"You don't," Cooper says now. "Fuck them, Eliza. Who cares if they have your dumb notebook? Let them post it online, no one cares."

"Easy for you to say," I say. "It's not your notebook."

"So you wrote some stuff in there about wanting to kiss Nigel when you were in ninth grade and how you're too shy to do karaoke, big deal," he says. "Just tell them to fuck off."

I take a deep breath and think about how easy it would be, how nice if I could just tell them I wasn't going to do it anymore, if I could just completely and totally not care. But I can't.

"I can't," I say. And for a second, I think maybe Cooper's looking out for me, that maybe he's worried about me, that even though what he did was gross and disgusting, that maybe he still kind of cares about me. He's getting closer to me now, looking at me, and he puts his arms on either side of me, holding on to the counter behind me with both hands.

"I miss you," he says, looking right into my eyes.

I want to say something smart back, but all I say is, "Then why are you letting them do this? Tell them to stop."

"Because if I try to call it off," he says, "if I stick up for you, they're going to want to go after you more. But *you* can stop them, you can tell them you're not going to do it."

"I can't," I say again. My heart is beating a million miles a minute, and a voice in the back of my head is telling me not to believe this, not to let him suck me back in again.

"Yes, you can," he says. "You don't have to make a fool of yourself."

And just like that, the spell is broken. I push Cooper away, then step to the side, out of Cooper's space, and whirl around.

"You think if I try to kiss Nigel I'm going to make a fool of myself? Why? Because Nigel's too good for me? Is that it?"

"No," Cooper says. He takes a step back, like maybe he's shocked by my outburst. "No, I wasn't saying that. I just meant that if you do this, then you're letting them —"

He cuts off and looks at something over my shoulder. I turn around and see Tyler walking through the entryway into the kitchen.

"Hey," he says, giving Cooper a nod. He makes his way over to the refrigerator and pulls a bottle of beer out. He opens it and takes a long swig, then wipes his mouth with the back of his hand. Eww.

"Hey," Cooper says. He turns his back on me and heads over to the fridge, where he follows Tyler's lead and pulls out a bottle of beer. Tyler looks at me then, taking me in, sizing me up.

"What are you doing in here?" Tyler asks me. "Don't you have a wannabe hip-hop god to try and kiss?" Then he laughs.

I feel the heat of tears prick at the back of my eyes, but I push them away. I don't have time to cry, and I don't have time to think about how easy it would be to tell them to go to hell, that I don't care if they put my stupid notebook on the internet. But I can't do that. Even if I wanted to, even if I didn't care. Because the thing is? Not all of the secrets in that book are mine.

Chapter Six

10:11 p.m.

Marissa's right — Nigel's over in the corner playing craps with
his friends, two guys I don't know very well, one named Nick
and the other one they just call Shove. I think it's because
he used to shove freshmen into lockers until someone ended
up with a broken finger and the whole administration really
started cracking down on that kind of stuff.

I smooth down my jeans and tell myself this is so totally
not a big deal. I mean, how hard is it really to seduce someone? Aren't all guys my age totally hormonal and just waiting for someone to even hint that they have a chance with
them? Of course, it would help if Nigel actually knew who
I was.

On the bright side, I'm definitely dressed for trying to

seduce someone. My jeans are tight, my shirt is low-cut, and my shoes are high.

I catch Marissa's eye as I make my way through the crowd over to where Nigel is—she's sitting on the L-shaped sofa, next to Jeremiah—and I see her send me a message with her eyes, "You okay?"

"Yeah," I telegraph back. As okay as I can be, anyway.

Nigel has his back to me, and he and his friends are all huddled around . . . hmm. Looks like they're huddled around nothing. Well, not nothing, exactly, they're huddled around the ground, which has a bunch of dollar bills on it, along with some dice. Nigel and his friends are really into craps, apparently. But I don't think it's the normal casino type of craps, it seems very shady what they do, with all sorts of weird rules. And of course they're not winning money from the casino, they're taking money from each other. Which is weird, you know, since they're all friends. But whatev. I'm not one to judge about what's weird or not, after the night I've been having.

I approach them gingerly, not really sure exactly where to begin. I mean, what do I say, "Oh, hi, Nigel, I have to kiss you now?," "Wanna make out?," or maybe just "I'll give you twenty dollars if you kiss me." I pull my shirt down a little, because I figure I need all the help I can get.

"Hello," I squeak at Nigel's back.

"Oohhs, yeah, you know I'm gonna school you fools," Nigel is saying. At least, I think that's what he's saying. It's hard to hear him, because he has his back to me.

"Hello!" I say again, a little louder this time.

Shove glances up from the other side of the circle, looks at me, and then goes back to ignoring me. Seriously, what is wrong with people? It was the same thing at Cure when I tried to dance with Rich. Am I that invisible?

I turn around and try to get Marissa's attention, but she's not on the couch anymore. I scan the room for her, or maybe even Clarice, who is supposed to be on her way, but the only person I see is Cooper, watching me from the other side of the room.

I turn back to Nigel and his friends and decide I'm just going to have to go for it. I lean into him from behind, so that my boobs are almost pushed against his shoulder, and then I whisper into his ear, "So how do you play?"

"What?" he asks, turning around and looking at me like I'm some kind of nuisance. Then his eyes fall on the plunging neckline of my shirt, and a flicker of interest passes across his face. Ugh. Of course. Although . . . I probably shouldn't look a gift horse in the mouth. I pull my shirt down a little more.

"I said, 'How do you play?'" I try to use my most seductive voice.

"You want to play?" Nigel asks incredulously.

"Aww, Nigel, come on," Shove says. He throws some dice into the middle of the circle. "You're up."

"You need a drink?" Nigel asks me.

"No," I say. "I already had one," I add. Nigel frowns. "Not that I'm, like, drunk or anything. I mean, I'm just . . . I'm like, loose, you know, like up for anything. But not so drunk that I don't know what I'm doing." I shoot him a smile, and Shove rolls his eyes at me like I obviously don't know what I'm doing.

Smart guy, that Shove.

"Why don't you sit right here," Nigel says. He moves over on the chair he's sitting on, a fold-up that can hardly hold him.

"Uh, thanks," I say. I slowly perch down next to him on the chair.

"Now watch and learn," he says. And so I do.

"Um, where are we going?" I ask thirty minutes later as Nigel leads me down the hallway of Isabella's apartment, to what I'm assuming is her bedroom.

"Down here," he says. The hallway is dim, and I'm trying to follow him, which is hard since I don't know exactly where I'm going, and these damn shoes are hard to walk in.

"Um, are we supposed to be back here?" I ask.

"It don't matter," Nigel says. Hmm. This definitely isn't true. I'm pretty sure Isabella is the type who doesn't like people hanging around her bedroom, poking through her stuff. Not that we're going to poke through her things. Like I even care. Probably all she has is a bunch of love letters to Cooper and sexy lingerie that she parades around in for him. I start to feel a little sick to my stomach, so I push that thought right out of my mind.

"Yeah, well the thing is," I say desperately, in an effort to keep Nigel at the party. "You know, I kind of feel like . . . dancing."

He turns around and looks at me. "You can dance for me, girl, you can give me my own private dance party."

Usually I'm a big fan of private dance parties. But something tells me Nigel has something different in mind than me dancing around by myself, pretending to be Beyoncé or Cher. (Yes, I pretend to be Cher—who cares? She's a survivor.)

"Yes, well, um . . ." The problem is this: I have to make sure that when I kiss Nigel, someone is around to see it. I don't think it's enough to make out in private. It has to be done somewhere semi-public. Damn. I should have kissed him while we were out in the living room. Of course, it's not like there were really any good opportunities. Nigel spent the whole time trying to teach me how to play craps, and I spent the whole time nodding at what he said, whispering things in his ear, and touching his arm a lot.

After a little while, Nigel stood up and said he needed a break (commence a bunch of eye rolling and complaints from Shove and the gang, who were super into the craps game), and then he started walking away, and I just sat there until he finally looked at me and said, "You coming?"

Now Nigel's opening the door to what appears to be Isabella's bedroom. The bed is neatly made in a lavender and white bedspread, and there's a tall white dresser in the corner. There's a huge floor-to-ceiling bookshelf against one wall, but it's, predictably, almost empty.

"Come here, Alyssa," Nigel says, patting the bed next to him.

"It's Eliza," I say, impressed he actually almost got my

name right on his own. Alyssa's pretty close to Eliza, right? And whatever, he knows it now.

"I think we should get back to the party," I say, glancing toward the door. Now that the moment is here, I'm nervous. This whole thing is so totally and completely bizarre when you think about it—I was so afraid to approach Nigel a couple of years ago, and now here he is, pretty much ready to make out with me. I mean, I could, like, *have my way with him.* If you'd told my two-years-ago self that, she would have been thrilled. Now all I want to do is run away.

Although . . . Nigel *is* hot. Not someone I'd want to date (the gambling problem, which seemed very edgy and cool in ninth grade seems kind of lame now, and the wannabe gangsta stuff got old a little while ago), but I've always loved his smile and scruffy face, and his hair is super-cute and spiky. Plus he has really broad shoulders. Much broader than Cooper's.

Maybe this is a blessing in disguise. I mean, maybe Nigel isn't going to be my future husband, but what if he's supposed to be my rebound hookup? Everyone needs a rebound hookup, right?

I make my way across the room and sit down next to him on Isabella's bed.

"Where," Nigel asks, lowering his eyes, "did you come from?"

I'm not sure if he means right now, or like, you know, into his life. So I just smile in what I hope is a mysterious way.

And then Nigel leans over and bites my lip. Wow. I've never had my lip bitten before. Not that I've had tons of hookups and tons of, um, chances to get my lip bitten. And not that it's horrible, getting your lip bitten. It's just . . . different. I decide maybe I should try to bite him back, but then his lips are on mine, and we're kissing.

Nigel's a good kisser. Not too soft, not too firm. He smells good, like cigarette smoke mixed with cologne—spicy and hot. He puts his hands into my hair and pulls me closer and then we're lying on the bed, and I can't believe it, but I am making out with Nigel Rickson! I let my fingers wander around the back of his neck and sort of . . . melt into him.

Hmm. Maybe there's something to this whole rebound thing after all. Or maybe I judged Nigel too harshly. I mean, I did like him once, and who said he can't be a good boyfriend? He'd be at least a much better boyfriend than Cooper. Although Cooper was a good boyfriend while he was my boyfriend, he was just faking it. And someone who's being real is a much better boyfriend than someone who is faking, no matter how amazing the faker is being.

Anyway, the point is that maybe Nigel *could* actually be my boyfriend, if I would just give him a chance, or he could at least be someone to hook up with more than once, not on a dare or anything, but—

Ooh. What was . . . ? Oh. Uh-oh. Nigel is getting a little, um, worked up.

He pulls me closer into him, and his mouth is on mine, but now he's a little more . . . insistent.

"Hey, hey," I say, pulling away and sitting up. I smooth my hair down. "Um, Nigel . . . let's . . . why don't we just chill out for a second."

Nigel looks upset, but then looks like he thinks better of it. "Why?" he says. He sits up and starts kissing my neck, and his mouth feels soft and warm against my skin. "Why do you want to chill out? Doesn't this feel good?"

"Ye-es," I say honestly. "But, um, I don't want . . . I mean, shouldn't we slow down a little bit?"

"Slow down?" Suddenly Nigel pulls back and looks at me like he's been slapped. "What do you mean, 'slow down'?"

"You know, slow down." He's stopped kissing my neck now, and I move a little closer to him, but he's not having it.

"I am not," he says forcefully, "a premature ejaculator." He looks at the floor and shakes his head.

"Oh, no!" I say quickly. "I don't think you're a . . . a premature ejaculator!"

"You don't?" he looks up at me. "Because I don't play that."

"No, I know you don't," I say. Geez. Talk about being defensive. Although. Now that I think about it, I do remember this rumor going around last year, something about Nigel and Hannah Rutherford, about how he got all worked up while they were making out and then he totally ruined her new comforter by —

There's a knock on the door and Nigel and I look at each other.

"Who is it?" I say.

99

"Yeah, who's there?" Nigel wants to know.

"It's Cooper," Cooper says. Probably coming to check up on me and see if I'm doing what I'm supposed to be doing.

Nigel looks at me. I shrug.

"Who?" he asks.

"Cooper Marriatti." The sound of the doorknob rattling fills the room. I didn't realize that Nigel locked the door. I'm not sure if I'm scared, flattered, or surprised that Nigel would think to do that.

"The room's full, dude," Nigel says. "Find your own." He smiles at me and I smile back tentatively.

But Cooper keeps knocking. "Eliza?" he asks. "Are you okay?"

Nigel looks at me. "That's your man?"

"No," I say, shaking my head. "That is *not* my man."

"Good," Nigel says. "Because I don't play that."

"I figured," I say, adding it to the list in my head of things Nigel doesn't "play." I clear my throat. "But you should know that he *is* my *ex*-man. Ex-boyfriend, I mean."

Nigel nods, like he can accept this.

"Eliza!" Cooper calls. "Open the door or I'm breaking it down."

"Oh, for Jesus' sake," Nigel says. He crosses the room and opens the door. "What do you want, dude? She's with me now. Bugger off."

Wow. Two guys fighting over me! Of course, one of them is fighting for me only because he wants to have sex with me, and the other one is fighting for me only so that he doesn't get into trouble with his secret underground jerky fraternity, but still. I sit up and pay attention to the drama.

"Eliza?" Cooper asks, looking past Nigel into the room. "Are you okay?"

Is he serious? Am I okay? He's blackmailing me and now he wants to know if I'M OKAY?

I get up off the bed and cross over to where Nigel is standing with the door open, his arm blocking Cooper's path into the room.

"I'm FINE," I say. "What's it to you?"

"Yeah," Nigel says. He slings his arm around me. "What's it to you?"

And then I realize I have a golden opportunity. I am standing in this room, with Nigel close, and Cooper watching. So I lean in really close to Nigel, grab his face, pull it toward me, and kiss him. Right on the lips, a full kiss, tongue and everything. And then I pull away to see Cooper's shocked expression.

"See?" Nigel says. "She's fine, mate."

And then Cooper turns around and walks away.

What. Ever. He was so totally just trying to see if I was making out with Nigel. So he could go back and report it to the 318s. He wasn't upset. Not for real, anyway. And honestly, it's so lame. I mean, he is a horrible, horrible person. And all that pretending he's concerned about me or that he wants to know if I'm okay? That just makes him worse, because an asshole who pretends to be nice? Is even worse than an ass-hole who actually is an asshole.

An asshole who sometimes pretends to be nice totally has the ability to suck you back in, making you think that you should give him another chance, or that maybe you had him all wrong.

Well! Not me! I will NOT even think for ONE SECOND that Cooper wanted to make sure I was okay, because if he was really that concerned with my well-being, he wouldn't be doing what he's doing.

"So . . ." Nigel says. He walks back over to the bed and pats the spot next to him. Oh, God. Now what am I going to do? It's obvious that he thinks we're going to pick up right where we left off.

"Nigel, listen," I say. "It's not that I don't—"

"I know, I know," Nigel says. "You don't want to go too far, just come sit near me, sweets. We can pick up right where we left off."

"I'm sorry," I say, shaking my head. "I just . . . I can't."

"Figures," he says, then gets up and stomps out of the room. He's mumbling something about not wanting to hook up with me anyway, how he can get any *bird* he wants. I think bird means "girl," but I'm not sure. Whatever. I slide my face into my hands. The warm feeling I got from the little bit of alcohol I drank is completely gone, and now I just feel . . . tired. And kind of sad.

I will not cry, I will not cry, I will not cry. I open my phone

and call Clarice, anxious to talk about her plan to get my notebook back.

"Where are you?" I ask when she answers.

"I just got here!" she says. "To Isabella's, I mean. It took
me forever, I completely forgot where she . . . Oh, eww,
some guy just vomited on the sidewalk outside of Isabella's
apartment." In the background, I hear sounds of . . . well.
Yeah. Someone is definitely vomiting outside of Isabella's
apartment.

"I'm in her room," I say. "Try to find Marissa and meet me
here."

Three minutes later, Clarice flounces in, followed by a
very perturbed looking Marissa. "Did you hook up with him?"
Marissa asks.

"Sort of," I say. Which isn't really true. For all intents and
purposes, I did hook up with him, but—

"Wait, hooked up with who?" Clarice wants to know.

"Nigel Rickson," I say.

"You . . . you had *sex* with him?" Clarice exclaims, her blue
eyes wide.

"No, God, I didn't have sex with him! Do you not know
me at all?"

"But you did hook up with him," Marissa says.

"I kissed him," I say. "That's all. Although to be honest, he
definitely wanted more."

Clarice nods in agreement, like this makes perfect sense. "I
heard he's a premature ejaculator," she says.

"Well," Marissa says. "I guess if you knew how easy it was going to be, you would have done it years ago."

"Not really," I say. Although maybe I would have. I mean, if I'd known, with one hundred percent certainty that Nigel wouldn't have turned me down, would I have? Tried to hook up with him? Maybe. Although it probably wouldn't have led anywhere, since Nigel is pretty lame with all his gambling and "I don't play that" nonsense. But I would have at least had fun.

Clarice is over at Isabella's dresser, and she picks up one of her perfume bottles and spritzes it on her wrist.

"Don't do that," I say. "They're not yours."

"Like Isabella cares," Clarice says, rolling her eyes. "She has about five million of them." She points to the array of bottles littering the dresser.

"So what's the plan?" Marissa asks. Her eyes are darting toward the door, and I can tell she wants to get back to Jeremiah. Jeremiah is kind of like a slippery fish; if you don't keep a tight hold on him, he can slip right through your hands. At least until he gets horny again. Then he surfaces right back up.

"Clarice," I say, standing up. "How can we get my notebook back?"

"I don't know," she says, shrugging.

I look at her blankly. "Didn't you say you thought we should steal it back?"

"Oh my God," Marissa says. "That is a *fabulous* idea. *You* came up with that?" She looks at Clarice like she can't believe it.

"Well, yeah," Clarice says. "But I don't have a plan to do it or anything. I don't even know where it is."

Jeremiah sticks his head into the room. "Hey," he says to Marissa. "Where did you disappear to?" He ignores me and Clarice. Wow. Way to be friendly. "Come back out to the living room, I need to show you something." And then he's gone.

Marissa looks at me, pleading. I sigh. She's no use to me right now anyway. "Go," I say, waving my hand. "I don't care."

She skips happily out the door.

"So what's the plan?" Clarice asks once Marissa's gone. She looks at herself in the mirror over Isabella's dresser. She gets a very serious look on her face, and then she asks, "Eliza, do you think I'm ugly?"

"What?" I ask. I lie back on Isabella's bed and wonder how this became my life. "No, Clarice, you are not ugly." I can't even begin to fathom that thought. Clarice has long blond hair and blue eyes and a very charming personality and guys fall all over themselves trying to hook up with her.

"Then why did Derrick kick me out of his apartment?"

"Um, because he's a guy?" I try. Something tells me getting into the whole "you're a tease" conversation right now isn't the best idea.

"I guess," Clarice says, abandoning her position at Isabella's dresser. She moves over to her closet.

My phone starts beeping, and I pull it out. A text from Kate. "HEY," she says. "MOM AND DAD TOLD ME THEY'RE OUT OF TOWN, HOW'S IT GOING?"

"GOOD!" I text back. "AT A SUPER-FUN PARTY WITH CLARICE AND MARISSA."

Maybe I should tell my sister what's going on. Maybe I should call her, let her know what the 318s are doing. Kate would definitely know what to do. Kate knows what to do in ANY situation, like last year when the guys started circulating that list and she started Lanesboro Losers.

That's the cool thing about Kate. She's not afraid to kick some ass when she needs to. And I'm sure she would be here in a second, kicking ass for me. But then I realize that the main problem is still the same. Some of the secrets in that book aren't just mine. Like how I wish I wasn't afraid to tell Marissa that Jeremiah is just hooking up with her and probably doesn't want to be her boyfriend. How I wish that I could tell Clarice that she shouldn't be such a tease. How I wish that sometimes, every once in a while, I didn't hate my sister because she's so perfect. Those secrets *cannot* come out. And the more people I involve in this, the greater the chances are of that happening. Besides. I don't want Kate kicking ass for me. That would be selling out.

There's a knock on the open door of Isabella's bedroom, and I look up to see Cooper standing there.

"Hey," he says. "I wanted to make sure you were okay."

"I'm FINE," I spit. "Stop asking me that! And it's not like you cared a few minutes ago. When Tyler saw us in the kitchen, you totally acted like his bitch."

Cooper looks at Clarice, who's standing in front of

Isabella's open closet. She has a dress in her hand, and she's holding it up to herself and posing Paris Hilton–style in front of the mirror. "Could you, uh, give us a minute?" Cooper says to Clarice.

"No," I say. "She cannot give us a minute."

"I don't mind," Clarice says reluctantly. She starts to put the dress back.

"She's staying," I say. "Why should she have to leave just because you decide you want to talk to me? She's my best friend."

"Because," Cooper says. "It's private. What I have to tell you is private." I look at his face, trying to decide if what he wants to talk about has to do with us (in which case he can go shove it, I'm in no mood to hear his dumb excuses and apologies), or if it has to do with the 318s and my notebook, in which case I probably should listen to him.

Clarice looks at me, and I nod. She puts the dress back in the closet and then scoots out the door.

"What?" I ask. I stand up from the bed and cross my arms.

"Look," he says. "You need to calm down. I'm not the enemy."

I stare at him incredulously. I almost can't talk I'm so mad. "You're not the enemy? Cooper, you're the reason I'm in this whole mess."

"I know," he says, running his hand through his hair. "Look, Eliza, I never meant to hurt you."

"You went out with me on a dare, and you never meant to hurt me?"

"It wasn't a dare," he says.

"It was an initiation prank! I mean, no, not *prank*, it was an initiation *rite* or something, which is pretty much the same thing as a dare."

"No, it wasn't," he says. "I mean, yes it was, but I never looked at it that way. I always thought that—"

"Oh my God!" I throw my hands up in the air. "You know what the problem is with you, Cooper?"

"What?" he asks.

"The problem with YOU is that you don't take RESPON-SIBILITY for anything! You think you can just run around, doing whatever you want to whoever you want, and that it's going to be fine. That everything is just going to be TAKEN CARE of for you, with no consequences."

"No, I don't," Cooper says. "And I *have* had consequences from what happened with me and you."

"Yeah?" I say. "Like what?"

He moves toward me, putting his hands on my arms. I try to pull away, but he holds them until I relax. I can feel the goose bumps starting up from his closeness, and I shiver as he pulls me closer. "I lost you," he says. "That was my consequence."

I lean my head against the hardness of his chest, and for one second, *one second*, I allow myself to believe him. I let myself believe that this is one of those cheesy teen movies where the guy starts dating the girl for no other reason than a dare, and then she gets a makeover and he decides he really does love her after all. But I haven't gotten a makeover, and this isn't a cheesy teen movie. In fact, it's kind of a nightmare. So I push him away. Hard.

"Stop," I say. "If this is one of your dumb tricks, I'm not about it."

"It's not a trick," Cooper says. "I miss you. If you'd just give me a chance, if we could talk, if you would let me explain—"

I push past him, heading for the door. I am so out of here. But what he says next stops me. "Eliza," he calls. "Look, I know where your notebook is."

I whirl around. "You do?" I search his face for any signs that he's lying, but if he is, he's doing a damn good job of it. Of course, he also convinced me for the whole of our relationship that he really liked me, so obviously I'm not the best at figuring out Cooper's bullshit.

"I do," he says. "It's at Tyler's house, in his basement. There's a whole area down there where we have our meetings." He walks over to me and leans in close, his breath on my ear, and another shiver goes through my body. "There's an open window that Tyler uses so that people can get in and out anytime they want without his parents knowing. You can slide through and get the notebook."

"Why should I believe you?" I ask.

"I'm telling the truth," he says. "And besides, what choice do you have?"

His lips are close to mine now, so close I could bite them if I want to, not that I do, I would never on purpose bite someone, that's just—

My phone beeps with a text from Kate.

"COOL!" it says. "I THINK I'M GOING TO STOP BY TOMORROW, HAVE A FUN NIGHT, LOVE YOU XXO."

Cooper squeezes my arm. "I better get out of here," he says. "I don't want them to see me with you." He looks at me and, for a second, I think I see longing in his eyes. "Be careful," he says.

And then he's gone.

Chapter Seven

11:17 p.m.

"Where are we going?" Clarice asks me a few minutes later as we walk down Newbury Street. "And why did we have to leave the party so quickly?"

"Because," I say, speeding up. I look up and down the street for Marissa. When I got back to Isabella's living room, she and Jeremiah were both gone. What is up with people disappearing tonight? It's so ridiculous, especially since the person who wants to disappear the most (me) can't.

"Slow down!" Clarice exclaims. "I'm wearing heels!" I don't point out that I'm wearing heels too, and that even though she has way more practice walking in them than I do (seriously — Clarice even has platform sneakers), I'm able to keep up the pace just fine. It's probably just because of the situation, and all the adrenaline coursing through my body. Kind of like how some mothers are able to just lift cars off their children.

Still. I slow down.

"Okay," I say. "Look." I pull her aside under an awning to a shop that's closed. "Cooper says he knows where the notebook is." Clarice's jaw drops, and then she jumps up and down and claps her hands. Apparently her feet don't hurt as much when she's jumping. Either that or she was being a total drama queen.

"Where is it?" she asks.

"He says it's at Tyler's house," I say. "But I don't know if I believe him."

"Right," Clarice says, narrowing her eyes. "Because he's a total shitsucker."

"Totally," I agree. "But on the other hand . . ." I sigh.

"We don't have any other kind of plan," she finishes.

"Right." We both stand in silence for a second, thinking about it.

"It doesn't really make sense for him to lie," she says. "I mean, why would he want to get you to Tyler's house?"

"So they could tie me up and kill me and/or force me to post the contents of my notebook myself?"

"No-o-o," she says. "That wouldn't happen. They're jerky high school boys, they're not killers."

"You obviously don't watch a lot of *Dateline*," I say.

"Honestly, Eliza, I don't think Cooper would lie to you. I think he still likes you. Like, for real likes you."

"No, he doesn't," I say, glaring at her.

"Okay," she says. She looks nervous and takes a step back. "If we're going, we need to figure out a way to get there, since Marissa has obviously ditched us." Across the street, two men in button-up shirts and jeans are standing outside a bar, and they tip their heads up in a gesture of "Hey, what's up?" and whistle at us. I smile back, but Clarice rolls her eyes.

"As if," she says to me. "I mean, they're, like, thirty." She starts walking and pulls me with her. "Besides, we don't have time for that."

"We need to find Marissa," I say, letting Clarice lead me down the street, "because without her, we can't go anywhere." We could probably take the T back to Newton, but it's a long ride, and we'd need a way to get to Tyler's house from the station. Which means we're going to need Marissa's car. Which reminds me. "Do you know where Tyler lives?"

"No," Clarice says. "I mean, I know he lives in Newton, but I don't know exactly where."

"Great," I say. Clarice is on her phone now, trying Marissa.

"Voice mail," she says. "She probably went somewhere with Jeremiah." She wrinkles her nose and then leaves a message. "Hi, Marissa," she says. "It's me again, we were just wondering where you are, you know, because you have the CAR and everything, and me and Eliza really have no way to get BACK HOME without you, so if you could give us a call that would be great, k, thanks, bye!" She ends the call. "Honestly, that girl," she says. "What is so great about Jeremiah Fisher?

You know, I used to have gym class with him sophomore year, and I'm not trying to be mean, but he really has this kind of, like, weird body-odor problem, and it's not even BO exactly, it's more of this weird musty smell, and I really hope he's gotten it under control because—"

A car pulls up next to us then, and the passenger-side window rolls down.

"Hey!" the driver says.

And then I notice the car. A brand-new red BMW that I would know anywhere, that I *should* know anywhere, because I spent, um, more than a few hours making out in the backseat. Cooper. WTF.

"I thought I told you," I say, "to stop following me."

"Get in, I'll drive you to Tyler's," he says. I look at Clarice. Clarice looks at me.

"No," I say. I grab Clarice and start dragging her down the sidewalk.

"But Elizzaaaa," she whines. "My feet hurt. And it's really cold out."

"It's not that cold out," I say, even though it kind of is and we're dressed completely inappropriately. "It's unseasonably warm for November. And besides, I don't care if we have to walk all the way back to Newton from here, we are NOT getting in his car."

"But we can't walk all the way back to Newton," she says, obviously missing the point. "Besides, we don't know the way."

"We'll look the directions up on your phone," I say. "Or we'll take the T back to Alewife and wait for Marissa."

"I've never used my phone as a GPS before. I don't know if it works." She looks doubtful. "Plus we don't know where Tyler lives."

"THEN WE'LL STOP AND ASK SOMEONE FOR DIRECTIONS!" I scream.

"Um, okay," she says, obviously deciding I'm not in a mood to be messed with. She gets quiet, but we keep walking, and then I realize that Cooper is still following us. He's driving really slowly against the curb, just about as fast as we're walking. You'd think more cars would be parked there, or that there'd be more traffic to block him, but no-o-o. He's totally able to car-stalk us.

"Go away," I say, leaning down and looking into the passenger-side window at him.

"Eliza, get in the car," he says. "This is crazy. Let me take you to Tyler's. And hurry up before someone sees us together."

"No," I say, and keep walking.

"Clarice?" Cooper pleads. "Don't you want to get in the nice warm car? I'll let you pick the music."

Gasp! That is totally hitting below the belt, since Clarice LOVES to pick the music in the car! And Cooper knows that Clarice loves to pick the music. He better not be trying to get all chummy with Clarice. We hate Cooper.

"No," I say. "We hate you."

"Eliza," Clarice whines. "Come on, he'll drive us back to Newton."

"We have a ride back to Newton," I point out. "Marissa's taking us." But my voice is already faltering.

"Do you see Marissa anywhere?" Clarice asks.

"No," I admit.

"And do you think she's coming back anytime soon?" Clarice raises her eyebrows at me. Damn. I know she's right. At last year's prom Marissa took off for, like, hours and didn't resurface until almost five in the morning. I still don't know what she was doing.

"No," I say. "But we can't just leave her." It's a last-ditch effort of a losing battle, and Clarice knows it. She looks at me incredulously, like she can't believe I've kept up the charade this long. "Fine," I say, sighing. I point my finger at her. "But don't you act nice to him."

"I would never," she says, looking offended at the thought.

But the second we're in the car, she leans over the front seat. "Coop," she says. "You know what I want."

Cooper plugs his iPhone into the car charger, opens up his Pandora, then scrolls through until he hits the listing for "Clarice's Jams," the station Clarice made for herself when Cooper and I were together. The sound of Fuel comes through the speakers, and Clarice settles happily into the backseat, texting away on her phone, probably with her cousin Jamie.

"What are we doing?" I demand.

"You want to go to Tyler's house, right?" Cooper asks. He starts heading back toward the Mass Pike, navigating down the super-narrow streets of Boston like a pro. "To try to get your notebook?"

"Yes," I say. "But how do I know it's really there? How do I know I can trust you?" I'm starting to sound like a broken record.

"Because you can," he says. "Why would I lie?"

"Why did you lie about any of the things you lied about?" I ask.

My phone vibrates. One new text. Tyler. "POST PICTURES OF YOURSELF IN A BIKINI ON LANESBORO LOSERS," it says. Oh, Jesus Christ.

On Lanesboro Losers, girls can create profiles too, with a photo gallery and everything. Only unlike the guys, girls are totally in control of their own information. I think Kate had intended it to be like, "Look at us, girl power, we're not afraid to post pictures of ourselves and our friends being happy" but that idea kind of . . . disintegrated. Girls started posting pictures of themselves very scantily dressed and used it in more of a "Look what you wish you could have" kind of way.

"Is that your next task?" Cooper asks.

"Yes," I say. Wait a minute. If I'm already getting what I'm supposed to do next, it means that the 318s must realize that I've completed the last thing they told me to do. "Did you tell them I made out with Nigel?" I ask Cooper.

"Yeah," he says. He shifts in his seat.

"Good," I say.

"Although I probably should have told them it shouldn't

117

count as a task, since you seemed to kind of like it." There's a sharpness in his voice, and if I didn't know better, I would think that Cooper was jealous. And then I remember. Cooper always had this . . . thing with Nigel. One night when we were all hanging out, Marissa let it slip that I used to like Nigel, and ever since then Cooper always seemed super-competitive with him.

"Oh, right," I say. "I forgot about how you're jealous of Nigel." I roll my window down and let the cool night air rush into the car, blowing my hair back from my face.

"Jealous? Of Nigel Rickson, are you kidding me?" Cooper signals and pulls onto the highway. "The kid wears his jeans so low you can see his boxers. How 1990s is that?"

"I think it's hot," I say. Which isn't totally a lie. I did think it was kind of hot at one point, and I'm not sure what I think about it now. Not totally hot, maybe, but it really doesn't bother me that much either. I mean, it's his *style*. He *owns* it.

"Are you kidding me?" Cooper says again. "So lame." He shakes his head. From the backseat, I can hear Clarice now on the phone, talking away. There's silence for a few minutes, punctuated only by Clarice saying, "I know . . . I know, totally."

Until finally, Cooper says, "Girls are crazy."

"Oh, hello, Random Thoughts That Make No Sense," I say. "I'm Eliza."

"I mean that girls are crazy if they think that Nigel Rickson is hot."

"He's a good kisser," I say.

"No, he isn't," Cooper says. He sounds shocked. I steal a

glance at him out of the corner of my eye. His eyebrows are knit together in concentration and confusion.

"How would you know?" I ask. "Have you kissed him?"

"No, I haven't kissed him," Cooper says, rolling his eyes.

"Then why did you say he wasn't a good kisser?"

"Because a guy like that knows nothing about what girls want."

"A guy like what?"

"A guy who says *dope* and *fly* and thinks he's Eminem," Cooper says.

"As opposed to a guy who drives a BMW and does whatever his dumb, super-lame friends think? That kind of guy really knows what girls want?"

That shuts him up for a second, and I turn and look out the window again. I think about how it used to feel to be in this car, when Cooper and I would go for rides, to anywhere and everywhere. We'd look up the best places to get ice cream on Yelp, then plug the address into his GPS and go, not caring if we had to drive for miles. We'd give all the sundaes points for taste, size, and flavor. And now . . . here I am, in the car for what is probably going to be the last time, ever, and it's for the worst reason ever, and that makes me really sad, and I hate myself for even being sad a little bit about it, because Cooper Marriatti is the biggest jerk in the whole world.

"Does this mean you're speaking to me?" Cooper wants to know.

"What do you mean?" I ask, turning back toward him.

His jaw is set in a straight line, and he's gripping the steering wheel with two hands, looking straight ahead.

"Well, last time I talked to you before tonight, you said you never wanted to speak to me again," he says. "And now you're speaking to me."

"I am speaking to you, out of necessity," I say. "Otherwise, no, I am not speaking to you."

"Ever again?"

"Ever again."

"Unless it's out of necessity?"

"Yes. I mean, no."

"No, you won't speak to me, even if it's out of necessity?"

"Yes, because I don't foresee any circumstances in which talking to you would be a necessity."

"None?"

"None."

"But I'll bet you didn't foresee this circumstance, so how can you really say for sure that you won't encounter another circumstance in which you will be forced to speak to me out of necessity?"

"I can't," I say. "But I *can* say with 99.999 percent accuracy that I will not be talking to you again, out of necessity or otherwise."

"But what if," he says, "I somehow became best friends with Nigel Rickson?"

"What if you did?" I say. "I would not want to talk to you even then."

"But what if you needed me to relay a message to him, like if you wanted him so badly that you just couldn't control yourself, and you needed him to know that you were lusting after him, and so you wanted me to tell him for you?"

"That would never happen," I say happily. "And if you want to know why, it's because I have already successfully hooked up with Nigel, and it took me about twenty minutes with no help from you, thank you very much."

"Okay," Cooper says agreeably. "But what if you and Nigel fall in love, and Nigel and I become BFFs, and then you guys get married, and Nigel wants me to be the best man, and you and I have to talk about the wedding plans?"

"That would never happen, because since Nigel would be so in love with me, he would have dumped you as a BFF as soon as we got engaged and/or told you you were not allowed to be best man at our wedding, per my wishes."

"Yes, but—"

"Wait a minute," I say. "Did you just say 'BFF'?"

"Yes," he says. He looks at me and shrugs. "I've been watching a lot of Disney Channel."

"Why?" I ask.

"Sarah's had it on a lot lately," he says. "And I don't have the heart to ask her to change the station." Sarah is his eleven-year-old sister. She is obsessed with all things Hannah Montana.

"Sounds fun," I say. I roll my eyes and try to sound all sarcastic, but the thing is, it kind of does sound fun. Hanging out with Cooper and his sister, who I adore, watching TV and eating snacks, lip-synching to Hannah Montana songs and critiquing her outfits. Not that Cooper lip-synchs to Hannah Montana songs. Although . . . he did do that JT song earlier like it was the most natural thing in the world. I glance at him out of the corner of my eye and try to picture him doing "The Climb."

"It's not as fun," he says, "as watching hip-hop videos with Nigel."

"Well, nothing is as fun as that," I say. "Nigel would teach me how to do all the hip-hop dances."

Cooper nods sagely. "Probably even crumping."

"Are you kidding?" I ask. "Especially crumping. That's, like, the staple of Nigel's dance knowledge."

Cooper looks at me and smiles, and I smile back. Are we flirting? Ohmigod. I think we are. For a second, I almost even forgot that Clarice was in the backseat. Which is definitely not a good sign. I can't just go around forgetting that my best friend is in the backseat; I'm supposed to be staying on task here.

And I definitely cannot just start flirting with Cooper, joking around with him about crumping and hip-hop dancing and all manner of tween shows on Disney!

I look at him suspiciously. This is just what he wants me to do! He wants me to lose my focus, he wants me to trust him, just like I did before, so that at the very moment he has me where he wants me, he can pull the rug out from under me and watch while it all goes crashing down.

I remind myself again that Cooper is despicable, that not only did he date me on a dare, he then turned me in to the school for what I wrote about him on the internet.

"So what's your next task?" Cooper asks. But I'm over it and not going to be nice anymore.

"Like you don't already know," I say snottily.

"I don't." We're in Newton now, and Cooper's signaling and pulling down a side street.

"Is this Tyler's street?" I ask.

"Yeah," Cooper says. "We're almost there." He's slowing down now. "So I'll probably just let you off at the top of the street, so that they don't catch us together."

"Fine," I say, mostly because I don't have any other choice.

"So what is it?" he asks.

"What's what?"

"What's the next thing you have to do?"

"Stop acting like you don't know," I say. "It's not you and me against them; it's all of you against me." From the backseat, I hear Clarice say, "Bye, Jamesers, kisses!"

"And Clarice is on my side too," I say proudly.

"Are we here?" she asks, leaning forward. "Thanks for the tunes, Coop."

"My pleasure," Cooper says.

"Stop being nice to him," I demand. "And yes, we're here. Well, we're sort of here." I look around at where we are. A nice, quiet street in nice, quiet Newton, where everyone has a golden retriever and all the houses look the same.

"Are you going to tell me or not?" Cooper asks, ignoring my remark about Clarice not being nice to him.

"Tell him what?" Clarice asks.

"What the 318s want me to do next."

"Oooh," she says, reaching into her purse for a piece of gum. "What do they want you to do next?" She holds out the pack of gum, and I take a slice. For a second, Clarice looks like she's thinking about offering one to Cooper, but I shoot her a look, and she puts the gum back into her purse without a word.

"Post pictures of myself on Lanesboro Losers," I say.

"But you already have a picture of yourself on LL," she says. "It's that really cute one that your mom took of you at the zoo last year." The picture in question is me, standing next to a llama who is leaning his head down next to me, licking my face. And it wasn't at the zoo, it was at this fair my mom dragged me to that just happened to have a petting zoo. For some reason she thought it would be super-funny to get a picture of me next to one of the animals, and the llama just happened to be the closest one.

"It wasn't at the *zoo*," I say. "It was a street fair."

Cooper snorts next to me, like he thinks it's funny.

"Shut up," I tell him.

"I think it's cute," he says. "The pic, I mean. Not the fact that you were at the zoo. Well, actually no, the zoo thing's cute too."

"Shut up," I say again. "I was NOT. AT. THE. ZOO. And anyway," I say to Clarice. "They want something a little more, uh, racy."

"Oooh," she says, nodding.

Cooper frowns. "What do you mean, racy?"

My phone rings then, and I check the caller ID. Marissa. "Hello?" I say.

"Eliza!" she says. "Oh my God, where have you been?" Which makes no sense, since we're the ones who've been looking for *her.* "I've been calling you for like three million minutes."

"I dunno," I say. "I've been right here, maybe my phone didn't have service or something."

"Well, what's going on? I got Clarice's message and I was trying to call her, but of course THAT didn't work."

"Marissa was trying to call you," I tell Clarice. She checks her phone.

"Oh," she says. "I guess I wasn't hearing the beeps while I was talking to Jamie."

Sigh.

"Anyway," I say. "We're at Tyler's house in Newton, trying to steal my notebook back."

"How did you get there?" she asks.

"Cooper drove us," I admit.

"What?!" she screeches. "That low-down, good-for-nothing jerk drove you there? Why?" She's yelling so loudly that I'm sure Cooper can hear her, but I don't even care.

"Um, because we couldn't find you," I say. "Where are you now?"

"I was with Jeremiah," she says. "Out on Isabella's terrace.

I'm so sorry, I thought you knew where I was! But he had to go home for a second, and so when I got your message, I started heading for home."

"We're on Elm Lane in Newton," I say. "Come meet."

"Be there in five," she says. She hangs up.

"She's going to come and meet us," I say.

"All right," Cooper says. "The more the merrier, I guess."

"Thanks for the permission," I say sarcastically.

It's not the most biting of remarks, but for some reason it seems to shut him up, and we all sit in silence for the next few minutes, waiting for Marissa. Well, except "Clarice's Jams," which is still pumping through the stereo system.

I watch the light streaming from a street lamp and try not to think about how I'm going to get the courage to post pictures of myself in a bikini on Lanesboro Losers. Instead, I think about how, if I can somehow figure out a way to get the notebook back, I won't have to do that.

Finally, after what seems like forever but is probably only a few minutes, headlights pull up behind us, and Marissa strolls up to Cooper's car.

"Hello, girls," she says. She ignores Cooper, which makes me happy.

"Hi," I say. I open the door and get out of the car.

"Hey," Cooper says, getting out as well. "Where are you going?"

"We're going to get my notebook back," I say. Honestly. Why am I so upset about him not being my boyfriend anymore? I mean, he's obviously ridiculously stupid. He doesn't even remember the plan and we just made it thirty minutes ago.

"I know that," he says. "But do you remember what I told you?"

"Yeah, about how his basement window is open," I say, waving my hand. "How hard can it be?"

"Okay, when you get to his house," he says, "there's going to be one window open, on the side of the house closest to us."

"Okay," I say.

"There will be a chair underneath the window, so step onto that to get down into the basement so that you don't get hurt. Once you're in there, go to the back corner—you'll see a circle of chairs, and in the middle of it will be a black box. Go into the box and get the notebook."

"Are you sure it's there?" Marissa asks, acknowledging him for the first time.

"Yeah," he says. "I'm sure."

"Wouldn't Tyler have it with him?" I ask. "So that he would know what to torture me with next?"

"No," he says. "He figured you'd probably at some point come up with the idea of getting it back, so he decided to keep it at home." He looks down at the ground. "He, uh, was afraid you might hire one of your sister's friends to kick his ass."

Hmm, now that I think about it, that's not that bad of an idea. "That's not that bad of an idea," I say. "Kate has a lot of friends on the football team, guys who do a lot of steroids and have rage problems. Guys who really need to take their aggression out on someone and would probably be happy to take it out on anyone who messed with me. For free, even." I look him right in the eye and hope he gets that I'm talking about him and not Tyler.

He doesn't say anything.

"All right," I say. "If this is a trick —"

"It's *not*," he says. He's looking right in my eyes, and I have no choice but to believe him.

"Now," I say, turning to Clarice and Marissa. "One of you is coming with me, and one of you is staying here."

"Why?" Marissa asks at the same time Clarice says, "I want to stay here."

"Because there's less chance of us getting caught if there's only two of us, and if this is a trick, one of you has to stay here so that she can tell the authorities all the pertinent information when the other two of us end up murdered and/or maimed."

Clarice gets a shocked look on her face, and her hands fly up to her nose. Clarice had a nose job a couple of years ago, and now she's super-paranoid about something bad happening to it that would mess it up. I guess a maiming qualifies.

Marissa, however, looks unperturbed. "Like they're going to kill us right in Tyler's house." She looks at Cooper, then walks over to him and pokes her finger right into his chest. "You better not be fucking with us."

He holds his hands up and takes a step back.

"Okay," she says, sliding the hair tie off her wrist. She

gathers her hair in a sloppy ponytail, slides her cell phone into her pocket, then hands her purse to Clarice. "You hold this while I'm gone."

"And don't be nice to Cooper," I command her. "And if you see anything weird, like if Tyler starts coming, or you get spooked by anything, anything at all, call my cell and warn us. Got it?"

"Got it," Clarice says. She gives me a determined nod but I'm still a little nervous.

Marissa and I start tromping down the street, looking out for Tyler's house, number 22.

"Jesus," I say. "That's number 223. Why the hell would Cooper park so far away?"

"Because," Marissa says, "he wanted to save his own ass of course, so he parked far away so that no one will see him. He doesn't give a crap if me and you have to walk and walk and walk." She doesn't seem tired, though, and she's taking long strides, so long that I'm struggling to keep up with her.

The houses go by faster than I thought, and before I know it, we're standing outside number 22, a white house with a huge sprawling porch with four rocking chairs on it.

"Why do they need so many rocking chairs?" I ask, frowning.

"Dunno," Marissa says. "Probably so they can all sit out there and pretend to be a big happy family and not even realize that their son is King of the Assholes."

"Probably," I agree. Now that I'm here, actually faced with the house and the task that's before us, I'm starting to lose my nerve. What seemed like a wonderful opportunity, something I could do to get out of this whole mess, now seems like a horrible, scary plan. I mean, think of all the things that could go wrong.

Then I notice that almost every light in Tyler's house is on, shining out into the night.

"All the lights are on," I whisper to Marissa.

"Yeah, so?" she says.

"So . . . maybe he's here."

"Nah," she says. "I saw him right before I was about to leave the city. He was still at Isabella's, hitting on some poor little freshman with a lip ring."

"But then . . . why are all the lights on?"

"Um, probably because his parents are home," Marissa says. "And because they're obviously not worried about their carbon footprint. Now, come on." She starts crossing the lawn, heading over to the side of the house where Cooper told us the open basement window is. I follow her, but . . . it's kind of creepy out here.

And dark, which in the city didn't seem so bad, because there were people around. And, yeah, some of those people were shady, but at least they were people. Out here there's just . . . nothing. But darkness. And crickets.

And okay, yeah, maybe Tyler's not here, but what if someone's about to jump out at me? Not even one of the 318s, but someone else? Like a real murderer or maimer, who's hanging out in the woods, waiting to get me? Not that there are woods out here. But Tyler's backyard *does* have a lot of trees and a lot of good hiding places for crazy people. Wouldn't that be a horrible, unfortunate coincidence? Some kind of weird stalker/killer type hanging out back here on the one night I attempt to break into Tyler's house?

"Hey," I whisper to Marissa. "Are we sure this is a good idea?"

"Do you want them passing your notebook all over school?" she asks.

"No," I say. "But they won't post it all over school if I do everything they say."

"How do you know?" She's a few steps ahead of me, and she looks over her shoulder meaningfully. Oh my God. I never even thought of that! I mean, there's no way to know for *sure* that the 318s are going to stop this. I could do everything they want, and they could still pass my notebook around or post it online. The only real way to make sure all the secrets stay safe is to get the notebook back.

"There it is," Marissa whispers. She points at the basement window, which, just like Cooper said, is open. Just a tiny bit, so little that you wouldn't even notice it if you didn't know. I guess that's the point. So that Tyler's parents and/or burglars don't realize that people can get in if they want.

There's no screen on the outside, and Marissa leans down and slides the window open easily. I take my cell phone out of my pocket and turn it on, letting the light flash into the cellar. There's a black folding chair under the window. Again, just like Cooper said.

"That thing doesn't look so sturdy," I say, looking at it doubtfully.

"Oh, please," Marissa says. "If it can hold Eric Partridge, it can hold us." Eric Partridge is one of Tyler's best friends, and he must weigh at least three hundred pounds. One time in gym class when we had to do rope climbing, Eric started climbing and the whole apparatus snapped and fell from the gym ceiling.

"I don't think Eric Partridge uses that chair," I say. My stomach turns a little bit at the thought of actually going into Tyler's basement. Isn't this breaking and entering?

"We're not going to get caught," Marissa says, as if she's reading my mind. "No one's going to hear us, we're going to get in and get out."

"Fine," I say uncertainly.

"I'll go in first," she offers. Which is really nice of her, since (a) it's my notebook that we're trying to get back and (b) we don't know for sure that there aren't snakes and/or someone waiting down there to kill us.

She turns around and slides down through the window, taking a second for her feet to find the chair. I hear her step down, and then she disappears into the darkness.

"Nice," she whispers. "It's carpeted."

I sigh and turn around, then slide myself backward through the window. My hands get wet grass all over them, and I'm pretty sure I shouldn't be doing this in the outfit I'm wearing. Hopefully Kate doesn't love these pants. My legs flail around until I feel the chair, and then I step down onto the carpet of Tyler's basement.

Marissa and I stand there for a second, letting our eyes adjust to the darkness. Hmm. Okay, so this place is starting to seem not so creepy. There are big squashy couches and a dart board on the wall. A big flat-screen TV is mounted in the corner, and a couple of empty beer bottles sit on a coffee table, which is littered with sports magazines.

The floor is clean, and it looks kind of like a bachelor pad, if the bachelor had someone (I'm assuming Tyler's mom) making sure that the place stayed clean and didn't get too gross. And it's not even really that dark down here, with the moonlight streaming in through the windows.

Over in the corner, near what looks like the furnace, is a circle of chairs.

"I think that's —," I start. From upstairs, a big booming sound comes, like someone dropped something on the floor. Then I hear a woman's voice say, "Oh sorry, Cal, I just wanted to make sure I got this in the fridge now that our guests have gone."

Ohmigod! Tyler's parents! Tyler's parents are in what sounds like the kitchen, and I can hear them! Talking about getting something into the refrigerator! I look over to the stairs that lead up to the house and notice that the door at the top of them is open just a crack. OH. MY. GOD. Is Cooper crazy? Why would he send me into Tyler's house if he knew that THE DOOR AT THE TOP OF THE STAIRS MIGHT BE

OPEN? And that Tyler's parents might be flouncing around the kitchen?

"Edward!" the woman's voice says next. "What are you doing up? It's very late, young man, you get back upstairs to bed right now."

"BUT I WANT WOOBY!" a little kid's voice (Tyler's brother?) screams. Yikes.

"Well, I don't know *where* your Wooby is, you probably . . ." the woman's voice fades away, along with the sounds of high heels clicking over a tile floor. I can hear soft classical music playing upstairs. Probably Tyler's parents had some kind of old people party or something, which is why they're still awake. And now apparently Tyler's little brother is awake too, looking for his Wooby.

Leave it to us to pick the one night there's a big commotion going on upstairs. I mean, parents should be in bed at this hour, sleeping or reading or watching *60 Minutes*.

I look at Marissa and put my finger to my lips, signaling her to be quiet. She gives me a look, as if to say, "Duh, I know." I start making my way slowly over to the corner, where the chairs are set up. In the middle of the circle I can see what looks like a box. A big black box. A big black box that probably has my notebook in it. A big black box that has a big black combination lock on it.

Shit, shit, shit. I crouch down and try to slide the top of the box back, but of course it doesn't open, and when I close my eyes for a second and will the lock to open, it doesn't happen.

"Shit," I whisper. I try to pick up the box, but it's way too heavy.

"What is it?" Marissa asks, tiptoeing over to me. "What's wrong?"

"It's locked." I'm punching Cooper's number into my phone. I cannot believe he would do something like this to me! Talk about sending me to the wolves!

"Eliza?" he asks when he answers. "What is it, what's wrong? Are you okay?" He sounds panicked, probably because he's afraid of getting into trouble with Tyler and the dumb 318s.

"You asshole," I hiss. "Why didn't you tell me it was locked?" From upstairs, the sound of a TV comes through the floorboards. It's muted, but sounds like some kind of late-night talk show. "And why didn't you tell me his parents would probably be up, basically partying in their kitchen?"

"I didn't know," he says.

"That it would be locked? Or that the parents would be up?"

Marissa, who's listening to my side of the conversation, sighs in exasperation.

"Either," he says. "But listen, it's okay, I know the combination. Twenty-eight, seventeen, seven."

I take a deep breath and start to turn the dial on the lock. But my hands are shaking, and I go by number 7, and so I have to start over. And then, right when I'm on the number 17 for the second time, the door at the top of the stairs starts to open.

Chapter Eight

12:18 a.m.

My stomach jumps into my throat, and I look over at Marissa, whose eyes become wide with fear. Shit, shit, shit. I put my finger to my lips and then don't move, hoping that whoever is at the top of the stairs is going to, you know, go away. Or at least decide they don't need whatever it is they wanted from the basement.

But then the light flips on, and we hear footsteps shuffling down the stairs, and suddenly a little boy appears. He's about six or seven, and he's wearing a pair of pajamas with planes all over them.

He's holding a book, and when he sees me and Marissa there, huddled over the box in the corner, he drops it on the ground.

"Oh, hi," Marissa whispers. "Hi, honey." She gives him a big smile. "We're friends of your brother."

The boy doesn't say anything. He just stares at us, his eyes wide.

"Yeah," I say, nodding. "We're friends of Tyler's, and I thought I forgot something here, but it turns out I didn't." Abandon plan! Abandon plan! Time to get the hell out of here.

Marissa and I are both moving back toward the window now, nodding as if that will make what we're saying true. Tyler's little brother (at least, I'm assuming that's who it is unless Tyler has some other reason for a seven-year-old kid to be living with him) is just watching us.

I catch Marissa's eye, and I can tell we're thinking the same thing—just get the hell out of here, and then we can worry about everything else later. It doesn't matter that we don't have the notebook, the most important thing is getting out of here without getting caught.

"So, um, we'll see you around, little buddy," Marissa says. She puts one foot on the chair and starts to climb up, but unfortunately, her upper body strength isn't that great, and she's unable to hoist herself back out the window. I guess Cooper forgot to take into account that we're girls, and that his dumb football-playing friends are probably lifting every single day, while I haven't lifted in . . . since . . . well, ever.

"Let me try," I say, after Marissa has tried six times unsuccessfully to lift herself up onto the ledge. Tyler's brother is still standing there, just staring at us.

But it's the same thing for me. I can't get up.

"Let me try to lift you," I suggest. "Then once you get outside, you can pull me out."

"Oooh, good idea," she says. I put my arms around her waist and lift with all my might. Marissa hauls herself up onto the ledge, and for a second, it looks like she's going to do it, she's going to get out, and yes, we don't have the notebook, but for a second it seems like we're going to be free, free, free.

And then Tyler's little brother takes a huge deep breath and screams bloody murder.

Tyler's mom is the first one to get down to the basement, and when she sees us, she freaks out.

"Cal!" she screams. "Cal, there are INTRUDERS IN OUR BASEMENT!" She picks up a broom from where it's leaning against the wall, and for a second it seems like maybe she's going to attack us with it. But then she thinks better of it, and just sort of stands there, brandishing it and looking threatening. She's all dressed up, in a black cocktail dress and high heels, so the whole thing is kind of funny. If it wasn't so serious, I mean.

"Oh, no," I say "We're not intruders. I mean, yes, we did intrude on your house, but we're not . . . I mean, we don't want to *take* anything." Lie, but sort of not really. We don't want to take anything that doesn't already belong to us, but something tells me that wouldn't go over well with this woman. "We're friends of Tyler's, and he told us we could come in through this window."

"Tyler would never say such a thing!" Mrs. Twill looks like she can't believe I would even suggest anything so outlandish. Shows how well she knows her son. "And especially not when he knows we were having the McIntyres over for dinner." She pulls Tyler's brother toward her. "You girls probably woke up Edward! His room is right over the basement!"

"I want my Wooby!" Edward yells.

"Of course, darling," Mrs. Twill says. She smoothes his hair and then looks around the basement. "There he is, over there on the couch." Edward scampers off and grabs a teddy bear off the couch, then buries his face back into his mother's dress.

"Anyway," Marissa says. "Tyler did say we could come in through the window. He told us to climb in, and to wait for him here." She shrugs and opens her eyes all innocent. I like where she's going with this, although I don't like her tone (kind of bitchy, which I think is the wrong tactic, since I can already tell Mrs. Twill is one of those mothers who doesn't think their kid can ever do anything wrong).

"It's true," I say, all sweetness and light. "He said to come in here and wait for him, that he'd be home soon. He said you guys didn't mind him having friends over late, but that he didn't want to disturb you and Mr. Twill and Edward. So we just came in, but we're so *so* sorry to scare you, I can't even imagine how horrible that must be, I know that I get super-scared when I'm home alone and I think like every single little noise is some kind of stranger creeping in, not that I'm home alone that much, but I am this weekend, my parents went away, so I can understand what you must feel like, coming down to the basement and seeing us here." I'm babbling now, but I can't stop.

Then Tyler's dad comes thundering down the stairs. "What's going on, Meg?" he asks. "Are you okay?" And then he sees us. "Oh," he says. He peers at us closely. "Eliza, right?"

"Yes!" I say, breathing a sigh of relief. Because I just remembered that Mr. Twill knows me! Well, sort of. I met him one time when he came to pick Tyler up from Cooper's house. He seemed nice enough, and we chatted for a few minutes about the weather and some football game he was excited about. He must be really good with names.

"You know her?" Mrs. Twill asks. She says it almost accusingly.

"This is Cooper's girlfriend," Mr. Twill says. "Right?"

"Yes, yes," I say, not bothering to correct him. "Yup, I'm Cooper's girlfriend all right."

"We haven't seen Cooper around here lately," Mr. Twill says. "What's he been up to these days?" Um, going out with me as a joke and then getting involved in some sort of cruel blackmail game involving your son and a weird notebook that I keep? "He's just been, you know, busy with school and stuff."

"Ahh," Mr. Twill says, putting his arm around Mrs. Twill. "Young love."

"Yup," I say. "We're young. And totally in love." I beam at him. Although now that I think about it, Mr. Twill's younglove theory might not be that far off. If Cooper isn't hanging out with me, and he's not hanging out with Tyler, then he's probably hanging out with Isabella. They're probably spending all their time at her dumb little apartment, pretending they're newlyweds or something.

"You're pretty," Edward says shyly to me.

"Thanks," I say, happy in spite of myself. I mean, how sweet.

"So, it's been great catching up, but obviously we've disrupted your night and I guess Tyler must not be coming home after all," Marissa says. "So we'll just be on our way out of here."

"Sure, sure," Mr. Twill says. "Come on upstairs and use the front door this time." He gives a big hearty laugh. "And we'll make sure we tell Tyler that you stopped by."

Marissa and I look at each other in horror.

"Actually, um, if you could . . . not do that, we'd really appreciate it."

Mrs. Twill narrows her eyes at us. She has short brown hair and a pointy nose, and when she narrows her eyes like that, she looks kind of like a chipmunk. But not in a cute way. More in a "I'm a deranged chipmunk that wants to maybe kill you" kind of way. "Why?" she asks suspiciously.

"Why?" I repeat, stalling for time.

"Yes," she says. "Why would we not tell Tyler you stopped by, if, in fact, he asked you to?" She still has the broom in her hands, and it's making me kind of nervous.

"Because," Marissa says. She still sounds a little haughty,

which really makes no sense, since we have no reason to be haughty. Like, at all.

"Because," I say slowly. "The thing is, Tyler didn't invite us here." Mrs. Twill gives us a smirk. Ugh. How annoying is she? No wonder Tyler is so misogynistic; he completely and totally hates his mother. "The thing is, that um, he just invited me."

Mr. Twill frowns. "Say what, now?"

"Well, Mr. Twill," I say, deciding that if there's any way out of this, it's with Tyler's dad and definitely not his mom.

"Please," he says, holding up his hand. "Call me Cal."

"Cal," I say, "The thing is that my friend Marissa here"—I point at Marissa—"she kind of has a thing for Tyler."

Marissa's eyes widen, and she opens her mouth to say something, but I shoot her a warning look. "Yes," she says morosely. "It's true. I have a thing for Tyler."

"A thing for him?" Mrs. Twill asks, looking slightly interested.

"Yes," I say. "She, you know, likes him." I rush on quickly before anyone can say anything else. "And since Tyler is one of the most popular and sought-after boys in our class, you can see how Marissa would be shy about telling him her feelings." I'm not sure which is more sickening—that Tyler's mom seems to be lapping up all these compliments about her son, or that, unfortunately, all the things I've said about Tyler are true. He *is* one of the most popular and sought-after boys in our grade.

"I get that," Cal says. "Tyler *is* kind of a ladies' man." He looks pleased. Maybe he's glad Tyler's getting a lot of ladies. Maybe he himself didn't do so well when he was in high school. Mr. Twill isn't bad looking, although he could stand to lose a few pounds. But his super-nice personality makes me think he might have been one of those nice guys who always finished last. I mean, he did end up with Mrs. Twill.

"Totally a ladies' man," I say, deciding to lay it on real thick. "In fact, if I didn't already have a boyfriend, I'm sure I'd be after him too."

"What's the point, though?" Mrs. Twill asks, all suspicious again. Wow. I guess it takes a constant stream of compliments to really distract her.

"The point *is*," I say, "that I brought Marissa here so that maybe she and Tyler could hang out. So that maybe he would get to know her, and that maybe they could start being friends."

"Yeah," Marissa says, nodding. "I really think that the basis of any strong relationship is a good friendship."

I nod. "I mean, right now they don't even talk," I say. "In fact, Tyler doesn't even know she exists."

"A pretty girl like you?" Cal asks. "I'm sure that's not true."

Mrs. Twill doesn't say anything, and I know she's thinking that there's no way Marissa is good enough for her son. Something tells me it wouldn't matter if Taylor Swift was standing here; Mrs. Twill still wouldn't think she was good enough for Tyler. It's really amazing just how clueless parents are about their own kids. I mean, Mrs. Twill obviously has no idea just what a complete and total idiot Tyler is.

"It is true," I say sadly. "Poor Marissa here hasn't even talked to Tyler once in her whole life." I put my arm around her and nudge her gently with my foot. In return, Marissa steps on mine. Hard. "Have you, Marissa?" I ask through gritted teeth.

"I haven't," she says.

"Which is why we don't really want Tyler to know we were here," I say. "Because if he knew Marissa was here, then he might want to know *why* she was here, and then he might ask me questions. Actually, knowing Tyler, he'd probably figure the whole thing out. About her secret crush, I mean. He is so, so smart."

"Probably," Mrs. Twill agrees. She slowly loosens her grip on the broom and then leans it back against the wall, which I think is a very good sign.

"Of course we wouldn't even dream of telling Tyler," Cal says. "But if Tyler knows what's good for him, I'm sure he'd be happy to have you as his girl."

"Thanks, Cal," I say, beaming at him. "So I guess we'll just be going then."

I start maneuvering around the Twill family, and we all start heading up the stairs, Cal in the lead.

"Now, you girls are more than welcome here anytime," he says.

"Mom, can I stay up and watch *Terminator*?" Edward's asking. Aww, how cute. He wants to watch *Terminator*. I love that kid!

"No," Mrs. Twill says. "You're going right back to bed!" Geez. Way to kill a buzz.

The door at the top of the stairs leads down a hallway and to the front door, and when we get there, I turn the knob and step onto the porch. The cool night air is a welcome relief, and I take in a big breath.

"Good night," I say, giving them a big wave. "Bye, Edward."

"Bye," Edward says, burying his face back in his mother's dress. Aww! He's shy around me because he thinks I'm so beautiful! Adorable, that little Edward. Too bad he has what seems to be some kind of inappropriate attachment to his mother. Hopefully he'll grow out of that before she ruins him the way she's obviously ruined Tyler.

"Bye," Marissa says.

I start down the porch steps, turning around once to see the whole Twill family standing in the doorway, their faces silhouetted by the light from inside.

We start walking down the hilled driveway, faster and faster. And that's when we see the flashing red lights of the police car, heading straight for us.

Chapter Nine

12:37 a.m.

The cop's name is Officer Clayborn, and he takes us back into Tyler's house, which really doesn't make any sense, since you'd think they'd want us *out* of Tyler's house, because, hello, we're in trouble for supposedly breaking and entering.

But Mrs. Twill gets all nervous about talking outside, because she doesn't want the neighbors to think there's anything going on. The way she says it makes me think that the cops have been at her house before, probably for something stupid Tyler's done, like last year when he and his friends went drag racing down on Route 128.

Anyway, apparently Cal called 911 from his phone before he came down to the basement and forgot to call them back and tell them never mind. Which, actually, probably wouldn't have worked since I'm pretty sure once you call 911 you can't really cancel it. It's, like, not allowed or something.

"Look, officer, it's just a misunderstanding," Cal says when we're all back inside, clustered around the Twills' kitchen table. "They're friends of my son's, and he gave them permission to be here."

"He gave them permission to break into your house?" Officer Clayborn asks. I know his name not because he told me, but because I can read his name badge. He's one of those super-hard-ass types, the kind that think it's their job to educate kids about how bad it is out there in the "real world."

"Yes," Marissa says, nodding. "It's because I have a crush on him." Oh, Jesus.

"He didn't tell us to break in," I say, giving Officer Clayborn my most dazzling smile. "He told us that we could get into his house through a window in his basement, and that we should wait for him there." I shrug my shoulders. "I have no idea what everyone's so upset about." I twirl a lock of hair around my finger and try to pretend I'm young and innocent. Which I am. Usually, anyway.

Officer Clayborn narrows his eyes. "Breaking and entering is a very serious offense, young lady," he says. Wow. Guess he's not going to be as easy to charm as my old pal Edward was. Edward, unfortunately, has been sent upstairs to bed. I guess they didn't want him to see what went down when law enforcement had to get involved.

"Oh, I know that," I say. "I know it's serious. Which is why I would *never* do it."

"They would never do it," Cal repeats. "Now, if there's nothing else you need, Officer Clayborn, I think it might be time to let these girls get on home." Of course, we're not really going home, but they definitely don't need to know that.

"We do need to get home," I say. "My parents are going to be worried."

"Totally." Marissa nods.

"I thought you said your parents were away for the weekend," Mrs. Twill says, apparently having a freakishly good and annoying memory.

"Uh, they are," I say. "But they like to call and check on me, you know, to make sure I'm doing okay."

"It's really cute," Marissa says. "They want to make sure she's all right, like, every second, since they know how nervous and fragile she is."

Officer Clayborn looks at us with steely, mean eyes. But there's nothing he can really do, even though I'm sure he'd love nothing more than to take us right down to the police station.

"You girls need a ride anywhere?" he asks.

"No, that's fine," Marissa says. "My car's outside, so . . ." We're moving toward the door now, and we're almost out of there, we're literally two steps away from getting onto the front porch, when it happens. Marissa's completely high and totally inappropriate shoes slip on Tyler's clearly just-waxed hallway, and she falls on her butt, her legs splaying every which way. And then a Ziploc bag of pot comes flying out from under her skirt and lands on the floor, right in front of Officer Clayborn.

Jeremiah gave it to her. Well, not really *gave* it to her. It was more like she stole it from him while they were hanging out, I guess to have something of his so he'd need to find her later. I think stealing a guy's drugs is like the modern-day equivalent of leaving something at his house so that you have an excuse to call him.

Anyway, it was hard to get the details with Officer Clayborn and the Twills standing right there. I kept telling Marissa to keep quiet, since I didn't want her to incriminate herself, but she kept blabbing away.

Finally, Officer Clayborn loaded her into the car and told her he was taking her down to the station. I felt completely horrible and kept insisting I should go with them, but for some reason, Officer Clayborn didn't want to hear it. Also, Cal kept saying things like, "Eliza would never allow illegal drugs to be brought into our home. I'm positive she didn't know about this, and there is no reason for her to get in trouble because of her friend's mistake!"

So after Officer Clayborn made me promise to drive Marissa's car back to her house for her, they left. Honestly, it's probably the scariest thing that's ever happened to me, so I can't even imagine what Marissa must be going through right now.

As soon as the police car is out of sight, I run back down the street to where Cooper is supposed to be waiting with Clarice.

"Did you get it?" Cooper asks from the driver's seat when he sees me. He shuts the book he was reading and tosses it into the back, then steps out of the car.

"No!" I scream. "No, I did NOT get it, and if you want to know why, it's because Tyler's parents caught us and now Marissa has been TAKEN AWAY BY THE POLICE AND IS PROBABLY GOING TO GO TO JAIL FOR DRUG POSSESSION!!"

"What?!" Cooper screeches.

"Where the hell is Clarice?" I say. We need to get away from Cooper and try to figure out a way to get Marissa out of jail. If that's even possible. I mean, I don't know anything about getting someone out of jail. And of course, there's the small problem of me having to post pictures of myself on Lanesboro Losers.

"Hey," I say to Cooper. "How do you get someone out of jail?"

"Well, it depends on why they're *in* jail," he says. "But usually you have to bail them out." Great. I'm totally broke. I have like maybe sixty bucks in my checking account.

"Where's Clarice?" I repeat, looking around for her. And then for the first time, I realize that Marissa's car is gone. It was parked right behind Cooper's, and now it's not there. And *then* I remember that Clarice had the keys. I turn to Cooper. "WHERE IS CLARICE?" I scream, all wild.

"She left," Cooper says. He looks nervous, like he's afraid I might start to freak out.

"She *left*?" I repeat incredulously. "What do you mean, '*She left*'?"

"She left," he says. "I tried to make her stay, but she said to tell you she was sorry, but she had to go. Some emergency with her cousin Jamie needing a ride. She wanted to text you, but she was afraid your phone might go off while you were in Tyler's house."

"Unbelievable!" I say. I pull my cell out and punch in Clarice's number. "And you just let her leave?"

"I told you, I couldn't stop her," Cooper says. "I tried, I swear, but she kept insisting it wouldn't take that long." He's leaning against the car now, his arms crossed over his chest.

"She's five foot two," I say. "You could have stopped her."

"You wanted me to use force to get Clarice to stay here and wait for you?"

"Not force," I say. "Your charming words. You can charm people into anything, Cooper, and then of course when it counts, you DON'T COME THROUGH!" I'm screaming again, and my voice is echoing up and down the empty street. Cooper looks really nervous now, like I might really go crazy.

My phone starts vibrating. One new text! I scroll the screen furiously, hoping it's Clarice or Marissa. But it's not. It's Tyler.

"REFRESHING YOUR PAGE ON LANESBORO LOSERS," it says.

"AND IT SEEMS AS IF THERE'S NOTHING THERE. YOU HAVE ONE HOUR AND THEN WE POST THE NOTEBOOK."

Oh. My. God. My legs start to feel all wobbly and my heart is beating super-fast, and before I know it, I'm sitting down. Right there, in the middle of the street. My legs just go all spaghetti-like, and I fall down to the ground and put my head in my hands. And then I start to cry.

"Hey, hey, hey," Cooper says. He crouches down next to me. For a second he doesn't say anything, and the sounds of my sobs fill the night air. Then, finally, he reaches over and starts rubbing my back.

"Don't do that," I say, but I don't try to get him to stop, either. Partly because it feels good and partly because I'm too exhausted to fight him.

"It's going to be okay," Cooper says.

"It's *not* going to be okay," I say. "My best friend is going to jail, my other best friend is missing, and I have to put pictures of myself up on Lanesboro Losers, and I just . . . I. Just. *Can't*." Suddenly the thought of taking pictures and posting them is totally and completely overwhelming. I'm spent, physically and emotionally. I just want to go home, curl up in bed, and never leave my bedroom, ever, ever again.

"Fine," Cooper says, standing up. "You're right. You can't do that. In fact, you're not doing that. You're telling him no."

"But then he's going to put my notebook up on the internet." I'm sniffling now, and I wipe my nose with the back of my hand. Gross.

"So let him," Cooper says. "Fuck him." He pulls his phone out of his pocket.

"What are you doing?" I ask, panicked.

"I'm calling him," Cooper says. "To tell him he better knock his shit off."

"No!" I say. I grab his phone out of his hand and end the call. "You are not going to call Tyler!"

"Why not?"

"Because if you piss him off, he's going to post my notebook, anyway. We can't do anything until we get the notebook back." Then I realize I just said we and I don't like it, so I correct myself. "I mean, until *I* get the notebook back."

"Fine," Cooper says. He slides the phone back into his pocket. He sighs and looks at me. "Okay, here's what we're going to do. I'm going to drive you to your house. And you're going to take pictures and post them on Lanesboro Losers. And then we're going to come up with a plan."

I look down at my hands. I look over at Cooper. I look around and see that I'm in the middle of Newton, in the middle of Tyler's street, with no real way to get home and no idea where home even is from here. I think about how one of my best friends is totally unaccounted for, and how the other one is in jail. And then I think about my notebook, and all the things that are in it. So when Cooper stands up and holds his hand out to me, I take it.

My house is quiet and dark when we pull into the driveway, which is a total relief. For some reason on the way over here,

I started having this paranoid idea that my parents might have decided to come home early. But the driveway is empty, and Cooper pulls his car into it and then follows me up the steps to the front porch.

"I'm going to go upstairs," I say, leading Cooper into the living room, "and take a picture of myself, and put it on Lanesboro Losers. You are going to sit down here and not touch anything."

"Okay," he agrees. He sinks into the couch in the living room and stares straight ahead at the wall. I bite my lip to keep from laughing. Because it's pretty cute.

"Here," I say, handing him the remote. "You can watch TV while you wait."

When I'm upstairs and in my room, I send Marissa a text asking if she's okay and telling her to call me as soon as she can. Then I send Clarice a text asking where she is and telling her to call me too. And *then* I open my closet and survey the contents. This whole bikini thing is going to be a challenge, mostly because, um, I don't really have a bikini. I mean, my idea of sexy is a tank top and a pair of shorts.

I paw through my bathing suits and consider just putting on one of my one-pieces, taking the picture and then slapping it up there, hoping for the best. I do have this red one that's kind of racy—super-low-cut on the top, super-high-cut on the bottom.

Or maybe I could just wear one of my regular bathing suits but, like, do something to up the sexiness factor to make up for it. Like get myself all wet in the shower or something. Or even in our hot tub. Of course, I have no idea how I'm going to take a picture of myself in the hot tub. And there's no way I'm letting Cooper see me in a bathing suit. I mean, yeah, when we were dating he saw, um, parts of me on a regular basis. But that was different. We're *not* dating now and, besides, who knows what kind of vulgar things he's said to the 318s about my body?

But if I don't do *exactly* what the 318s say, they might consider it cheating, and I really, really don't want that to happen. They'd probably come up with some kind of punishment task, where I had to, like, pose nude or something. Ugh. The fact that the 318s are making me do this shows just what complete and total scumbags they are. It's disgusting, when you think about it.

I take a deep breath and then head into Kate's room, hoping I can find a bathing suit of hers that fits me. I finally find an old bikini shoved way in the back of one of her drawers that might work. It's black (very slimming!), with a crisscross top and a bottom that's high-cut on the side.

I just hope that I can fit into it. I take my clothes off, reminding myself that it doesn't matter what I look like, that I just need to post the pictures and get my notebook back. Then I can delete it and no one will ever see it again. Well. Unless someone decides to right-click and save it, but if that happens, there's really nothing I can do about it.

I step into the bottom of the suit, and it seems to fit, but the top is giving me a hard time. I can't figure out how to tie the straps behind my head, because they're crisscross and very skinny, and my hands are shaking, which isn't helping.

"Eliza?" I hear Cooper call my name from the top of the stairs. The top of the stairs, as in, he's right outside my sister's bedroom. I freeze. "Are you okay?" he asks.

"Yeah," I say. "I'm fine, just please don't—"

The bedroom door opens then, and Cooper's standing there. And he sees me. With the bikini bottom on and the top of the bikini hanging off me. I turn around quickly so he can't see anything else.

"Get out!" I yell.

"Okay, okay!" he says, and shuts the door. "Sorry!"

I take a deep breath and try to still my beating heart. Then I reach around and start trying to tie the top again, but it's not working. And when I finally do get it tied, I look in the mirror and see that it's all weird, with everything kind of smushed together. Definitely not a flattering look. And for once, it's not my body that's the culprit.

Dilemma: Do I leave it like it is, and deal with the smushed boobs, or untie it and try to get it right?

Cooper knocks softly on the door. "You okay?" he asks.

"I'm fine," I say. I grab a T-shirt out of one of my sister's drawers, pull it over my head, and open the door. I decide to pretend that moment never happened, the one where Cooper almost saw me topless. "I told you to wait downstairs." But I say it all happy and pleasant, so that he doesn't know I'm rattled.

"I know. I just wanted to make sure you were okay." His hands are in his pockets, and he looks sincere. For a second, I remember how nice it was when he was rubbing my back a little while ago, and I'm tempted to break down again, to tell him no, I'm *not* okay, that this whole thing sucks. But instead I force myself to push past him.

"I'm fine," I say, heading into my room across the hall so that I can get my digital camera.

"Did you take the pictures?" Cooper asks.

"Not yet," I say. "I'm going to take them by the hot tub."

"Oh." But he says it kind of . . . strangely. Like it's a big effort for him to get the word out.

I leave Cooper back in the living room, then head outside to the backyard and turn the hot tub jets on. I've decided to pose by the hot tub not because it's super-sexy (that's just an added bonus), but because I figure it will be a good way to cover up my body. If I can just take a picture of myself where half of my body is out of the water, I won't have to worry about everyone seeing my bottom half. Genius, right?

But when I get into the water, it soon becomes pretty clear my plan is not going to work. Every time I try to take a picture of myself, all you can see is my head. And when I angle the camera down, it looks like I'm trying to take a pic right down the front of my bathing suit.

You can also totally tell that I'm taking the pics myself, which make them seem all "Look at me, I'm taking a sexy pic of myself" instead of an "Oh, look, someone just happened to take a pic of me in the hot tub while we were all hanging out and I just happened to look very sexy." Not to mention the whole, uh, boob-smushing issue. And, yeah, I don't plan on keeping these pics up for that long, but still. Do I really want to give the 318s something else to laugh at me about?

I take a deep breath. "Cooper?" I yell. "Can, um, you come out here?"

Cooper's on his cell phone when he comes outside, and he puts a finger to his lips.

"Sick," he says. "Are you serious? . . . Yeah, totally, dude."

He must be on the phone with Tyler. I reach for my phone, which is sitting on the side of the tub, and check to see if Marissa or Clarice have texted me, but they haven't. So I lean back in the tub and close my eyes, letting the hot frothy water slide over me, and hope that it somehow calms me down.

"Yeah, I'm just on my way back to Isabella's, had to go on a beer run," he says. "See you soon." He shuts the phone.

"I have about an hour before I have to be back to Izzy's," he says. "Tyler wanted to know where I was. I can stall him a little bit, but . . ." Ewww. Izzy? I have never heard anyone call Isabella "Izzy" before, which means it's some kind of dumb nickname that he dreamed up for her. I want to kill him, and instead I have to allow him to take pictures of me in a bikini, which I will then have to post on the internet for my whole school and possibly the world to see. Talk about your nightmare scenarios.

"Izzy?" I say. "You call her Izzy?"

"Well, not all the time," he says. "Just, you know, some-times."

"That's really stupid," I tell him. "And, just so you know, I don't need you out here anymore, so go away."

"How are you going to take a picture of yourself, then?" he asks. "It looks like you're having some trouble."

"No, I'm not," I lie. The steam from the hot tub is now fog-ging up the lens of the camera, and I try to wipe it off, but my hands are all wet and I end up just smearing the condensation around. The camera gets all slippery and I almost drop it into the water, and so finally Cooper comes over and takes it out of my hands.

"I got it," he says. When his fingers brush mine, my stom-ach flips, and I hate, hate, hate that he can still have that effect on me after everything he's done.

"Fine," I say. "Let's get this over with." I make sure the bubbles are covering up pretty much everything and give a smile.

Cooper lowers the camera and frowns. "That's your big sexy pose?"

"Yes," I say, nodding. "I'm wet, I'm in a hot tub, I'm wear-ing a bikini." I check all the things off. "Those are three very sexy things."

"Yes," Cooper says. "Those are three very sexy things, but, um, we can't see your bikini."

"I've decided that maybe we should leave some things to

the imagination," I say. "Like less is more." This is contradictory to what I said before, about not wanting to incur Tyler's wrath by cheating, but that was before Cooper got involved in the actual picture-taking part of this whole process.

Cooper looks a little uncertain. "I guess," he says. He takes another picture of me and then comes over and shows me the pic in the view screen. Even I'm surprised at how lame it is. I look like I'm on a family vacation or something, and that if you panned out, you'd see a bunch of old people around me, like maybe I went to go visit my grandma at her retirement home or something and ended up in the hot tub with her and her friends. Totally lame and not sexy at all. You can't even see the bathing suit.

"Good pics," I say in a strangled voice.

Cooper raises his eyebrows.

"Fine," I say. "A little more cleavage." I take a deep breath. "But could you, uh, could you retie my strings?"

I turn my back to him and lift myself out of the water, then reach up and untie my strings. I lean over and hold the front of the bikini top close to my chest. Cooper has no trouble tying the strings the right way (Maybe he does it for "Izzy"?), and his fingers brush against my wet skin, making me shiver.

When he's done, he goes back to the front of the hot tub. I slide back into the water and take another deep breath, then lean back and look up at the sky, letting the warm night air pass over my face. Then I sit back up very, very slowly until the very top of my bikini is showing. Cooper snaps a picture, and his face is totally blank, so I stand up just a tiny bit more, so that my boobs are totally out of the water, and you can see the top of my stomach. That should be fine, right? And not too crazy. It just looks like I was relaxing in the hot tub and now I'm getting out, and someone just *happened* to snap a pic of me while I was doing so. The water's still covering a lot, but you can clearly tell I'm wearing a bikini.

And then Cooper's eyes get wide. Like, really, really wide.

"What's wrong?" I ask, quickly sliding back into the water. "Was it really horrible?" I wonder if I can Photoshop. Not that I've ever used Photoshop. But I know it can work miracles. Whenever they show those pics in magazines of how celebrities get their pictures retouched, you can totally tell the difference.

"No," Cooper says. "It was, uh, it was good." He seems flustered.

"Let me see," I demand.

He brings the camera over to me, and I look at the preview screen. Wow. I actually don't look that bad. I'm leaning over the water, and you can see the top of my bathing suit. Since it's Kate's, it's of course a little tight, and so my cleavage looks amazing. My hair is all wet, and I look a little nervous, but kind of in an alluring way. "Wow," I say.

"Yeah," Cooper says. He puts the camera down and looks at me. Is he . . . Is Cooper . . . Oh. My. God. Cooper thinks I look hot! Cooper Marriatti is actually enjoying taking pictures of me. Ugh. Typical guy. Of course, now that I know that, I might as well have a little bit of fun with it.

"I don't know if it's sexy enough," I say suddenly. "I think I need to do a few more. Maybe one like this." I pull myself almost completely out of the hot tub and lean my head back, letting the water from my hair slide down my back.

"I think I got enough," Cooper squeaks. He comes over and hands me back the camera, and this time, when our hands touch, it feels like a hot current is passing between us.

"Are you sure?" I ask innocently. "I was showing off my chest, I know, but I thought we could do some more, like where I could let the rest of my body be—"

"I'm sure," he says.

I click through the pictures, deleting all the earlier ones off my camera, so that I'm left with the one that just shows me standing up in the water.

"So now what?" Cooper asks.

"Now we head up to my room and post this online," I say. I pull myself out of the hot bubbly water, and the cool night air moves over my skin, making me shiver. Cooper grabs a towel off the chair next to the tub and wraps it around my shoulders.

"Thanks," I say. He doesn't move his hands right away, and I'm not sure if it's my imagination, but I feel like he pulls the towel tighter than he needs to for a second, like maybe he doesn't want to let me go. But just like that, the moment's gone, and my phone is ringing.

Marissa. "Oh, thank God," I say when I answer it. "Where are you? Are you okay?"

"I'm fine," she says. "I think they just wanted to scare me

a little bit, they called my parents, and they had to, um, come down to pick me up."

"Were they pissed?" I asked.

"What do you think?" she asks. "Anyway, they're taking me to come and get my car. Where are you guys?"

Uh-oh. "Um, well, I'm at my house," I say. "With Cooper."

"They're at Eliza's," I hear her say to her parents.

"But Clarice isn't here," I say. "She took your car and went to help her cousin Jamie with something."

There's silence on the other end of the line. Obviously Marissa is trying to figure out just how to tell her parents that Clarice has her car, and that she has no idea where she's gone.

Finally she just says, "Oh, Clarice will just bring my car home for me? So that my parents don't even have to go and get it? That is so-o-o-o nice of her, make sure you thank her for me. Okay, byyye!" And then she clicks off.

"Her parents picked her up," I say, a little dazed. "She's in trouble, I think, but I'm not sure if—"

My phone vibrates in my hand. One new text. Marissa. "CALL ME WHEN U MEET BACK UP W/ CLARICE, AND THEN COME AND GET ME!"

I text back, "AREN'T U IN TROUBLE FOR UR IMPENDING DRUG POSSESSION CHARGES?"

"WILL SNEAK OUT, CALL ME," comes the rapid reply.

I sigh and rub my temples. Okay. Time to focus.

Chapter Ten

1:47 a.m.

Cooper follows me into my room and pulls up a chair next to my computer, uninvited. I don't say anything, but when I go to log on to my Lanesboro Losers account, I glance over at him. "Don't look," I instruct. "I don't want you to see my password." This is mostly because my password is *Cooper143* which means "Cooper I love you" in text speak. In my defense, I totally made that password like ages ago, and I just, you know, haven't gotten around to changing it. I'm very lazy like that.

"I'm not looking," Cooper says, plugging the digital camera into the back of my laptop. "You know, this would be a lot easier if Lanesboro Losers had the ability to get uploads right from people's phones, then we wouldn't have to—" He breaks off as he see me staring at him incredulously.

"You're giving me advice on how to make Lanesboro Losers better?" I ask. I mean, yeah, I know Cooper's into some of that techy geek stuff, but still. Now's kind of a weird time to start talking website features. Especially for a website that is kind of a big part of the weird mess we're in right now. I mean, that *I'm* in.

He frowns. "Well, no, not you. Your sister. She's the one in charge of it, right? Or at least makes the decisions on what new features to add and stuff?"

"Yeah, I guess," I say. "I mean, she still has control over all of it, even though she's not really actively involved with it anymore."

"Okay, so then why wouldn't I tell you how I think it could be better?"

"Well, because from what you've told me, this site is pretty much responsible for not only ruining my night, but possibly my life. Also, it ruined yours. So it doesn't make any sense that you would be all for improving it."

Cooper shrugs. "It didn't really ruin my life." He looks at me, his green eyes serious. "I didn't really want to go to Brown, you know that." I nod. He doesn't. Want to go to Brown, I mean. And I do know it, not because he's ever said it, but because I could just tell from the way he talked about it. Kind of . . . passionless.

I think he might really want to go to NYU, which is supposedly his safety school. They have a great computer department, and I know he's always wanted to live in New York

City. But his parents want to keep him close to home. His mom thinks living in New York City is crazy. Plus, both his mom and dad went to Brown, and so they think he'll be happy there.

"It was kind of a blessing that I didn't get in," he says.

"So then why are we going through this whole charade?" I ask, frustrated. "If you don't even care about Brown."

"I told you, this wasn't my idea," Cooper says. "It was Tyler's."

"Oh, that's right," I say. "I forgot. You do everything Tyler says." I mean for it to come out snotty, but instead it comes out half-snotty, half-sad.

"That's not true," he says.

"If you didn't care so much about Brown, then why did you file a complaint with the school?" I ask. "About what I wrote?"

Cooper sighs, his green eyes crinkling at the sides. "I didn't," he says. "I told you, that was Tyler. And, Eliza, honestly, I —"

"I don't want to hear it," I say. And it's true. I don't want to hear his dumb excuses for how he's so sorry, and it was just a joke, and he never meant to hurt me, and blah blah blah. I click around on the computer and upload the picture, reminding myself that I'm not supposed to cry over him for one more second. And definitely not in front of him, that would be completely and totally unacceptable.

Once the picture is uploaded and posted, I turn and look at Cooper.

"What now?" I ask.

"I don't know, I guess we wait." He looks at his watch. "I'll have to leave within the next ten minutes or so though. I need to get back to Izzy's."

"Oh, right, Izzy's," I say. "You wouldn't want to keep her waiting, that would just be horrible for the poor thing, she might die without her boyfriend for two whole hours." I put on a fake shocked expression.

"Her boyfriend?" Cooper frowns. "Izzy's not my girlfriend."

"Well, then you should probably have a talk with her," I say. "Because she most definitely thinks she's your girlfriend."

Cooper's frown deepens. "No, she doesn't."

"Yes," I say. "She does. In fact, she told me tonight on the T." Although that's not exactly true. I mean, she didn't come out and say, "Cooper is my boyfriend, woo!" But she definitely implied it, I mean, she was doing everything short of getting his name tattooed all over her, like a big "COOPER AND ISABELLA FOREVER AND EVER" in a heart or something.

"She's not my girlfriend," Cooper says again.

"Really?" I ask. "Then why were you watching her party?"

"She asked me to," he says, shrugging. "We're working on a project together for psych class, so I was over there last night." I give him a skeptical look. "We're just *friends,* I swear. I've never even kissed her." He holds his cell phone out to me. "Do you want to call her right now and ask her?"

"No," I say. "Whatever, I don't really care." Which isn't

true. I do care. A lot. Now that I know he isn't hooking up with Isabella, I can almost let myself believe that maybe he does really miss me. I *could*, but I won't.

"Eliza—"

"Stop," I say, holding my hand up.

"You don't even know what I was going to say!"

"Yes, I do," I say. "You were going to say how you never meant to hurt me, and how the whole thing just got out of hand, and how you're a really nice guy who would never do something like that to me on purpose, and OMG peer pressure."

"'OMG peer pressure'?" Cooper repeats.

"Yeah," I say.

"I don't know what that means."

"It MEANS that you are going to say it was all peer pressure that made you do what you did." Honestly!

"What does *OMG* mean?"

"Oh my God."

"So you think I was going to say 'oh my God' peer pressure?" Cooper asks. He's looking at me the way he used to look at me, with this cute little half smile that makes me feel like whatever I'm saying is adorable.

"No, I think you were going to say a bunch of bullshit about peer pressure and how it pertains to what you did to me, and my 'OMG' was symbolic of all the bullshit you were getting ready to spew at me."

"Oh." The half smile leaves his face.

"That's all you have to say? Oh?"

"No." He sits down on my bed and then swivels my desk chair around so that I'm facing him. I look down at the ground. He takes my face in his hands and tilts my chin up so that I'm looking at him.

"Stop," I say. But I don't really move. I can't move. It's like I'm stuck, and I can't get away from him. Okay, that's not really true. I *can* move, there's nothing, like, *wrong* with me or anything. But I kind of like the way his fingers feel on my face.

"Stop what?" he asks.

"You're not allowed to tilt my chin," I say. "You lost that right when you broke up with me."

"*You* broke up with *me*," he says.

I guess technically he's right. I broke up with him as soon as I found out what he was doing, as soon as I found out that there was a list, a disgusting list filled with things that were disgusting, of points and things that he would get for getting me to go further with him.

"You lost the right to tilt my chin when we broke up, then," I correct myself.

"Okay," he says. But he doesn't move. Now his finger is drawing little swirls across my chin and onto my cheeks and over my lips.

"You're still doing it," I tell him.

"I never wanted to break up with you," he says.

"Of course not," I say. "Because being broken up with means you got caught."

"No," he says. "That's not why."

I shiver a little, and then move my eyes up so that I'm looking at him. "If that's true," I say, swallowing, "then why didn't you fight for me?"

"What do you mean?"

"You could have fought for me, you could have tried to get me to change my mind, you could have followed me the night I found the list."

His eyes shift to the side then, and the spell is broken. Because he knows it's true. If he really wanted to be with me, he would have fought for me. He would have tried to chase me, he would have tried to be with me, he would have tried to change my mind, he would have told Tyler that he didn't want to be in the 318s anymore. But he didn't. Because everything Cooper tells me is a complete and total lie, always.

"Eliza," he says finally. "Why do you think you ended up on that list?"

"What list?" I ask, frowning.

"The list of the girls that were eligible for our initiation task?"

"There was a list?" I say, pushing the chair back from him and wheeling myself away. "A list of girls that were eligible? For you to *fake-date*?" Seriously! Just when I think he can't sink any lower!

"Yeah," he says. He's hunched over now, his elbows resting on his knees. "I thought you knew that."

"No, I did not know that!" I say, throwing my hands up. "And I have no idea how I got on that list! Probably because

I'm quiet, or because I don't have a perfect body, or maybe because I'm Kate's sister and in your warped, dumb little minds you guys thought that would be funny."

"No," Cooper says. "You were on that list because I wanted you on it." He says it like this should make me happy. I look at him. Cooper might be insane. Seriously.

"Oh, great," I say. "That's a wonderful reason, that really makes me like you a lot better, Cooper. Thanks so much for clearing that up."

"No," he says, shaking his head. "I mean, I wanted you on it because I wanted a reason to talk to you."

"Oh my God," I say, standing up out of my chair, furious. "Are you seriously that delusional? You think that you saying you wanted to date me as a joke because you wanted to get to know me better makes me feel any better? If anything, it just makes it SO. MUCH. WORSE." I look him right in the eye. "You disgust me," I say. "Now get out of my room."

"What?" he stands up and looks at me. "Did you not hear what I just said? I said that I wanted you on that list because I found you interesting, and cute, and I wanted an excuse to talk to you."

He takes a couple of steps toward me, but I step backward, away from him.

"And that was your idea of a good excuse?" I say. "To put me on a list of girls you guys thought it would be funny to use?" I'm almost crying now, and I do NOT want to cry in front of him, so I turn around so he can't see my face. "Go," I say softly. "Please, just get out of my room."

There's silence for a minute, and neither one of us moves.

"Eliza—"

"I'm SERIOUS," I say. "GO."

"Fine," he says softly. He stops when he gets to the door. "Um, do you mean just get out of your room, or get out of the whole house?"

I think about it. "Well, preferably the whole house, but I might need a ride from you, so don't go just yet."

My cell phone rings then. Clarice. I pick up the phone. "Hiii," she trills, like nothing's wrong, and she didn't just steal Marissa's car and leave me stranded at Tyler's with no way home.

I'm already all worked up because of my fight with Cooper, and so it starts to come out in the phone call. "What the *hell* is going on?" I ask. "Why did you just abandon me and Marissa?" I start pacing back and forth, I guess because I have all this nervous energy that needs to come out.

"What do you mean?" Clarice asks. "I had to go and pick up Jamie. Honestly, it was horrible. Madeline left her at this arcade in Southie and, Eliza, you know Southie is NOT a good part of town."

"She couldn't take the T?" I ask. "To get home?"

"The T doesn't run this late," Clarice reports. "And besides, Jamie doesn't take the T."

"What do you mean, 'Jamie doesn't take the T'?" I repeat.

Who doesn't take the T? It's like saying you live in New York and don't take the subway. Although. I guess there are a lot of people who live in New York and don't take the subway. A lot of rich, snobby people who are always taking cabs. "Let me rephrase that," I say. "What kind of person doesn't take the T to get out of a bad neighborhood?" It's totally counterintuitive, when you think about it. Not taking public transportation because you're afraid of it, yet risking your life in a bad part of town? Although I'm sure they were exaggerating about how much danger they were in. Clarice's cousins Jamie and Madeline are always exaggerating things.

"Jamie and Madeline don't," Clarice says. "And she was so scared, I really wish you would have heard her."

"I'm sure she was really scared," I say, still pacing and trying to keep control of myself so that I don't lose it completely. Cooper's still standing by the door, trying not to laugh, which is just annoying me even more, because I know why he's laughing.

Cooper met Jamie and Madeline once, at this cookout he had. Clarice just showed up with them, and we couldn't exactly ask them to leave, even though they were kind of weird. They spent the whole time under these huge umbrellas they brought because "their delicate skin couldn't take the sun's ultraviolet, ultra-cruel rays."

Later, we surmised that they must have a thing with umbrellas, because when Cooper served them drinks, they produced pastel-colored paper umbrellas for their glasses out of their purses and then sat by the pool, under their umbrellas, sipping away happily and talking only to each other.

I shoot Cooper a death glare now and curse myself for ever letting him get so invested in my life. What was I thinking? We were only together for a couple of months! It was a horrible plan to let him meet my friends and spend so much time with them.

"She was totally scared," Clarice is saying. "They were showing a boxing match on one of those big screens there, and you know how Jamie gets about violence."

"Why did she go there in the first place?" I ask.

"She was dared," Clarice reports. "She lost a bet."

"She lost a bet and so she had to go to an arcade in Southie?" Then I realize I'm getting too caught up in the details of Jamie's life, when I have much bigger things going on. "Never mind," I say to Clarice. "Look, where are you?"

My phone vibrates in my hand and beeps, cutting off her answer. "Hold on," I say. "I have a text."

I check my phone. "SAW THE PICS," Tyler says. "NOT BAD. NOW GET BACK TO THE CITY BY 3 AM TO GET YOUR NEXT TASK."

Jesus. How late is this going to go? And when are they going to JUST STOP ALREADY? I take a deep breath. "Clarice," I say calmly. "Where are you?"

"Um, I'm leaving the city right now." Shit, shit, shit. She's never going to have enough time to get me and then bring me back there by three o'clock. "Okay," I say. "Can you go and grab Marissa at her house?"

"Marissa went home?" Clarice asks. "That wasn't very nice, Eliza. She shouldn't have left you."

"Marissa *didn't* leave me," I say. Has Clarice forgotten her recent carjacking? "*You* left. You left us all alone."

"No," she says. "I left you with Cooper. Where is Cooper, anyway?"

"He's right here," I say, looking at him warily.

"Hi, Clarice!" Cooper yells.

"Hi, Cooper," Clarice yells back. Ugh. But I really don't have time to get into a big discussion about her loyalties, so I'm forced to let it go.

"Look," I say. "Marissa got arrested."

"Marissa what?!" Clarice exclaims.

"She'll explain everything to you when you see her," I say. "Call her first, because she's going to have to sneak out. Tyler wants me back in the city by three, so go and get her, and then meet me at the Perk on Newbury." Perk is this all-night coffee place that usually gets pretty busy on weekends after everything else is closed. I figure it's a good place to meet, since it's in a safe area, and there should be at least *some* people around.

"Got it," Clarice says, and then she clicks off.

I look over to where Cooper is sitting. "So," I say. "Uh, you want to take me with you, back to Boston?"

He grins. Ugh.

I make him wait in the living room while I change into comfortable jeans and a soft gray sweater. Then I head downstairs and follow him angrily and silently out of the house and back into his car.

The whole ride into the city, we don't talk. Which is fine with me. There's hardly any traffic, and so we're able to get in fairly quickly, and I spend the whole time pretending to be texting on my phone. Cooper lets me pick the music, so I create a pop station on Pandora and keep the music up a little too loud for conversation.

The weird thing? I kind of do want to talk to him. Okay, that's not true. I want *him* to want to talk to *me*. I know I told him to go away in my bedroom, and for the most part, I did want him to go away. I mean, I *do* want him to go away. My brain won't let me believe anything that he says. But the other, smaller part of me wants him to talk to me again, to bring up the fact that maybe he wasn't completely and totally doing what Tyler told him to, that maybe a small part of him still cares about me. Even though I know it's stupid.

Which is why I have the music on. Because I know if I start talking, I'm going to try to steer the conversation around to why he wanted me on that list and what he thinks about everything, and I know that's just dumb. Kate always told me that you should judge people by their actions and not their words.

And so far, Cooper's actions definitely prove that he could care less about me. I mean, all he would have to do to prove it would be to get my notebook back for me. Or to quit the 318s. Or to at least kiss me.

But if he doesn't care about me at all, if he's such a big jerk, then why is he helping me so much? I steal a look at him out of the corner of my eye. I try not to admire the way his hair fades into the back of his neck, the way his green eyes are all droopy and brooding. I try not to stare at his forearms clutching the steering wheel. Cooper has very sexy forearms. I think about those arms around my waist, and I swallow hard and then shift my gaze and look back out the window. Honestly, I never should have trusted anyone who's that good-looking.

When we take the exit off the Mass Pike to get into Boston, Cooper reaches over and turns the radio down.

"Um," he says. "Where should I . . . I mean, I have to get back to Isabella's, so should I just bring you to Perk?"

Right. Isabella's. I totally forgot about that. That's a whole other story. I mean, it's a little bit better now that I know Cooper's not with her. But still.

"Yes," I say. "You can drop me off at the Perk on Newbury."

"I'm glad you picked that place," he says. "That's a safe area."

"Thanks for thinking of me," I say sarcastically.

His hands tighten around the steering wheel. "What's that supposed to mean?" he asks.

"It just means," I say, "that if you were really so concerned about me, you wouldn't just dump me off at Perk and then rush off to Isabella's."

"Eliza, I told you," he says. "Isabella and I are just friends.

The only reason I'm even going back to her apartment is so Tyler won't know that I'm with you."

"I am so sick of all this Tyler bullshit! Honestly, Cooper, you really need to get some balls."

"I have balls," he says, looking pissed.

"No, you don't."

"Yes, I do," he says.

"No, you don't," I say.

"I can't believe this," he says. "I was all set to call him and tell him you weren't going to play along with him anymore! Remember? When we were outside of Tyler's and you started crying? *You're* the one who told me I shouldn't!"

Hmm. Good point. But whatever. I am too mad to even speak to him. We're on Newbury Street now, and Cooper's moving down the street, stopping every so often so people can cross. All the bars have just closed, so there are a lot of people on the street, heading back to their cars or looking for a place to get a late-night bite to eat.

"Look," Cooper says, "I'm sorry you think that I'm not on your side, but I've been helping you all night, so a little bit of gratitude would be appreciated."

I look at him incredulously. "A little bit of *gratitude*?" Is he serious? "You're the one who got me into this predicament in the first place! If it wasn't for you, I'd be at home right now, with Marissa and Clarice, completely happy and enjoying the fact that my parents were out of town by ordering pizza and watching whatever movies I wanted On Demand and having a great time!"

"Oh, yeah, that sounds like you're really missing out on a lot," Cooper says.

"Well, maybe it doesn't sound as exciting as making out with girls for sport, but I happen to like it," I say.

"Eliza," Cooper says. He reaches over and tries to take my hand, but I pull it out of his grip.

"Whatever, Cooper," I say. "If you really want to help me, then please just stay far, far away from me."

He's stopped at a crosswalk, and so I don't even wait for him to say anything. I just step out of the car and onto the street.

Chapter Eleven

2:41 a.m.

I'm so shaken that once I'm out of Cooper's car, I start walking the wrong way down the street, away from Perk. I don't want Cooper to see me turning around, because that would be super-embarrassing, so instead I just keep walking and then turn down a side street so I can walk around the block.

When I finally *do* get to Perk, my head feels a little bit clearer, and my heart rate's slowed just a little bit. Still, I'm super-wired, so I opt for an herbal tea that the barista recommends when I ask for the best caffeine-free, calming drink available. I find a little table in the corner and sit down, wishing I had a book or a newspaper or some knitting or something to do while I sit here.

I take a sip of my tea. Eww. Kind of gross. Very strong

and herby, with not enough milk and sugar. But if I want to put more in, it means I have to go back up to the counter, and then I'll lose my table. And if I lose my table, then I'll really be in trouble, because what will I do then? Just walk up and down the street with my drink? I can't exactly window-shop; all that's open now are a couple of twenty-four-hour restaurants and pizza joints.

I sip my tea and feel sorry for myself for a little while, then flip open my phone and call Marissa.

"Hello!" she says when she answers. I can tell she's in the car, because I can hear the rush of the wind behind her, like all the windows are open. "What's going on?"

"Where are you guys?" I ask.

"Hold on," she says. "I can't hear you." She turns the music down, and then says something to Clarice, giggling. Great. It sounds like they're having a grand old time, with music and the wind blowing their hair, and I'm sitting here drinking some dumb herbal tea that tastes like pinecones, all by myself and waiting for the next thing I have to do that is going to humiliate me.

"Okay, sorry," Marissa says, coming back on the line. "Clarice just picked me up."

"You should have seen her, Eliza," Clarice yells. "She had to jump off her back deck; she almost killed herself."

"Yeah, real funny," Marissa says. "Anyway, where are you?"

"I'm here," I say, "at a table in the back."

"We're almost there," Marissa says. "See you in five."

Fifteen agonizing minutes later, they come waltzing in, giggling and laughing and falling all over each other, chattering away. Since when did those two become such good friends?

"Hi," I say morosely. "What took you so long?"

"Sorry," Marissa says. "I made the mistake of letting Clarice drive, and so of course we had to circle around forever, looking for a parking spot that was big enough for her to pull into, since she's totally afraid to parallel park."

"I'm not afraid," Clarice protests. "I just don't trust myself to do it, and I knew you'd get super-upset if I ended up scratching your car." She flips her blond hair over her shoulder. "But anyway, it didn't even matter, because a nice man totally parked the car for me."

"A nice man parked your car for you?" Honestly, you couldn't even make this stuff up.

"Yes," Clarice says. "He was crossing the street, and I saw a spot, and so I said, 'Excuse me, sir, but would you possibly be willing to park my car for me?' and so he did!" She beams.

"Why didn't you just do it?" I ask Marissa.

"Because I wanted to see what was going to happen," Marissa explains.

"How did you know the guy would be a good parallel parker?" I ask Clarice.

"He just had that look about him," she says.

"What if he was drunk or something?"

"Eliza, he wasn't drunk!" She looks shocked. "He was

wearing a suit and he had a very well-groomed beard!" I decide not to point out that if he was wearing a suit, that probably meant he hadn't been home from work to change, which most likely meant he'd been prowling the streets of Boston since he got out of work, maybe even since yesterday, doing God knows what.

"He *might* have been a little drunk," Marissa says. "And he *did* ask for your number."

"He was fine," Clarice says dismissively. "He was just a nice old man who wanted to do a good deed for someone in trouble."

"Anyway," I say. Although it's kind of comforting, just how naive Clarice really is.

"Yeah, anyway," Marissa says. She plops down in the chair across from me. "So what are we doing? What's the deal, what's the plan?"

"I dunno," I say, shrugging. "I'm waiting to hear from Tyler."

"Okay," Clarice says. "Then I guess we should probably go get drinks."

"Don't get herbal tea," I tell them, wrinkling my nose. "No matter who recommends it."

"Got it." They head to the counter, and I try to take another sip of my tea.

My cell phone starts ringing. Cooper! I guess he didn't listen when I told him to just leave me alone. I hesitate, wondering if I should answer it, if maybe he's calling to tell me what it is I have to do next. But then I decide no. If they really want to get in touch with me, they can have Tyler text me. And a second later, my phone vibrates and the new text notification goes off. I look down at the screen. Tyler.

"TELL KATE THE TRUTH ABOUT WHAT HAPPENED WITH MIGUEL CONTADOR."

I look down at the text and blink. Shit, shit, shit. Out of all the things in my notebook for them to make me do, this one just might be the worst.

Marissa and Clarice come back to the table, each with a huge plastic-domed cup filled with something cold. Clarice licks some whipped cream off her spoon and sits down daintily in the seat across from me, and then Marissa sits down next to her.

"You were right," she says. "They totally tried to give me the herbal tea. I told them, 'No thank you, I need a caffeine jolt.'" She looks at me. "What are you staring at?"

I'm looking down at the table, to where my cell phone is still in my hand. Marissa reaches over and grabs it. "Tell Kate the truth about what happened with Miguel Contador," she reads out loud. Her eyes get wide, and she looks at me.

"Uh-oh," she says.

"Yeah," I say. "Uh-oh." Although *uh-oh* is pretty much an understatement.

Clarice frowns and her blue eyes flash with confusion. "I don't get it," she says. "Who's Miguel Contador?"

"Miguel Contador," I say. "You remember him, he was a senior when we were sophomores."

"Sort of," she says, frowning. "Did he have dark hair and dark eyes?"

"Yes," I say. "He was always, um . . ." I swallow, remembering. "He was always working out."

"So what happened?" Clarice asks. "With you and Miguel Contador? And why do you have to tell Kate about it?" She dips her straw back into the whipped cream on top of her drink and sucks it off daintily.

Marissa and I glance at each other.

"Well," I say slowly. "Um, Kate was a junior when I was a freshman."

"Duh," Clarice says. "I'm not that bad at math."

"Well, uh, Miguel was her boyfriend," I say.

"They dated for, like, four or five months," Marissa adds.

"Wait," Clarice says. She sets her spoon down on the table and looks at us. "How is it that Marissa knows this scandalous story you're about to tell, and I don't?"

"How do you know it's going to be scandalous?" I ask.

"Because," Clarice says, sounding exasperated, "if it wasn't scandalous, then (a) it wouldn't be a secret, (b) I would know about it, and (c) the 318s wouldn't be making you do something having to do with it." I blink at her, impressed by her astuteness. She is, of course, right on all counts.

"Um," I say. "Well, you're right on all counts."

"Eliza hooked up with him!" Marissa blurts suddenly,

unable to contain herself. Then she claps her hand over her mouth, but she totally doesn't look even remotely sorry. "Oops," she says.

"Eliza!" Clarice yells. "You hooked up with your sister's boyfriend?!" A couple of people turn to look. This place is surprisingly busy for such a late hour.

"Yes," I say, blushing. "But it wasn't my fault, it was . . . Kate had this huge party at our house while my parents were out of town, and Miguel was there, and everyone was in the hot tub and swimming and he . . . he had these abs that were like . . . he was always working out," I finish lamely.

"So because he was always working out, you thought it was okay to hook up with him?" I should have known Clarice wouldn't take this story well, what with her stringent views on love and romance.

"No," I say. "I didn't think it was okay to hook up with him! But he and Kate hadn't been going out for that long, and earlier she'd told me that she wasn't sure she really liked him."

"Sounds like you're trying to justify it," Clarice says, wagging her finger at me. "That's not good, Eliza."

I sigh and decide I'm going to have to tell her the whole story.

What happened was, Kate and I had been getting ready for the party earlier that night, both doing our hair in the same bathroom. One of us could have gone downstairs, but we liked getting ready together. Kate would tell me what kind of makeup I should wear, and then she would do my hair, blowing it out until it was super-straight and shiny.

Kate had been dating Miguel for a couple of weeks, and they were in that stage where you kind of have to decide if it's really going anywhere. At least Kate thought that's the stage they were in, because I remember her telling me that she wasn't so sure if she really liked him all that much.

When she said that, I was a little shocked. This was Miguel Contador we were talking about. He was definitely considered a catch at our school, with his dark skin and perfect smile and even more perfect body. (Seriously, I know I keep talking about it, but his body was absolutely sick. Totally chiseled, but in a natural-looking way, not in an "I do steroids and am a huge muscle head" kind of way.)

And yeah, I'll admit it. I was a little bit jealous. I was fifteen, and Miguel was almost eighteen, which seemed so old to me at the time. And I couldn't for the life of me figure out how or why Kate could just be so cavalier about the whole thing! I mean, she just announced that she didn't know if she really liked him, kind of like she was announcing she didn't know what to order at the Burger King drive-through or something. It was shocking. And, I admit it now, a little bit annoying.

I didn't say anything, but later that night, when I found myself alone with Miguel in the family room, I remembered what she had said. The TV was on, flashing some MTV show or something, and I was in there watching it because I had started feeling a little hot outside, like maybe I'd had a little too much to drink. So I came inside to cool off, and then Miguel came in a few minutes later. He was fresh out of the hot tub and toweling himself off.

"Hey, Kate's little sister," he said.

"Hey," I said. I still got nervous around him, even though he was now Kate's sort-of boyfriend, and every time I'd talked to him he'd always been super-nice. He sat down next to me, and I don't really remember exactly what happened next, but I know we started talking, and I remember making some comment about how he had the same last name as the famous cyclist Alberto Contador. And Miguel looked at me kind of like I might be nuts and said, "Who the fuck is Alberto Contador?" Which was kind of funny in a sad, tragic sort of way since I'd been super-proud of myself when I'd found out that little tidbit of trivia, and I had squirreled it away for days, waiting for the perfect time to pull it out and impress him. I didn't even like cycling.

I remember him asking me about Kate, about if she ever talked about him, if she really liked him, and then I started getting annoyed, thinking about Kate and how she didn't even care if Miguel liked her or not. Anyway, I don't remember exactly what I said, but I think Miguel was getting the sense that maybe Kate didn't like him as much as he liked her.

And I'm not sure if he was trying to get back at her, or if he just felt sorry for me or what, but the next thing I knew, he leaned over and he was brushing his lips against mine, and I'd never kissed anyone before and I didn't have time to think about if I was doing it right or not, because he opened his mouth and then I opened mine, and we kissed for a few seconds.

Then someone called him back outside, and he left, and Kate must have won him over and decided that she really did like him after all, because he was her boyfriend for five months after that. I never told her what happened. Miguel and I never talked about it, and as far as I know, he never cheated on my sister or kissed anyone else while they were together.

"Well, that's why I didn't know about it," Clarice says, after I'm finished telling the story. "Because I didn't live here yet." She shoots Marissa a smile, as if to say, See! That's the only reason you knew and I didn't!

"That's all you're worried about?" Marissa asks her incredulously. "That you didn't know the secret because you didn't live here yet?"

"It makes me feel better," Clarice explains, "to know there's a reason I was being kept out of the loop." Their bickering actually cheers me up a little. I mean, at least there's something normal going on.

"Well, does it make you feel better," Marissa asks, "that now Eliza has to tell Kate what happened?"

My phone goes off again. "Tell her in person," it says. "Bring Kate to the Perk near BU and tell her there."

"What the hell?" I show the phone to Clarice and Marissa.

"Don't they know we're already at a Perk?" Clarice asks. "It would have been so much better if Kate could just come and meet us here." She sighs.

"They probably want you to go there," Marissa says, "because they're going to send someone to listen in on your convo."

"Why would they do that?" I ask, frowning.

"Because they want to make sure you really tell her. Otherwise, where's the proof?"

Hmm. She's probably right. What. The. Hell. Not only do I have to confess something to Kate that's going to be really, really hard, but now I have to do it with one of Tyler's dumb minions hanging around, probably jeering and laughing in my face or something. Maybe he'll even send Cooper. Plus, it's three in the morning. What the hell is Kate gonna think when I show up at her dorm so late?

"It'll be fine," Marissa says. She reaches over and rubs my shoulder. "I promise." But I really, really don't believe her.

Chapter Twelve

3:15 a.m.

We drive over to Boston University, and we all stay pretty quiet on the drive over, I think mostly because we're sick and tired of all this running around. Plus, you know, up until now things haven't been that crazy, what they've been asking me to do. Like, there haven't really been that many big life-changing repercussions. But now . . . I don't want to think what could happen.

I call Kate on the way, half hoping she'll be asleep or won't pick up her phone. But she answers on the third ring, sounding wide awake.

"Hey," I say, trying to infuse my voice with as much normalcy as possible. "It's me. Did I wake you up?"

"No, I'm up," she says. "I have this super-huge paper due on Monday, so I'm pulling an all-nighter."

"Oh," I say. "That sucks. Um, is it okay if I come over for a little while?"

"Okkkkaaaay," she says. "What's wrong?" This makes me feel even worse, since I know she's asking not because she's surprised I'm coming over (I go over to her dorm room a lot, actually), but because it's three in the morning and she can tell from my voice that's something not right. Also, although she sounds worried about me, I can tell she's happy to hear from me and happy that I'm coming over, which makes me feel like a complete and total shit.

"Um, nothing's wrong," I say. "I just . . . I need to talk to you about something."

"At three in the morning?" she asks.

"I was kind of in the neighborhood," I say, "for a party." Which isn't a lie. I *was* in the neighborhood for a party earlier.

"Is this about Cooper?" Kate asks. "Honestly, Eliza, if you need me to get someone to talk to him, I will." Again I consider just telling Kate the truth. The whole truth, about how Cooper and the 318s have my notebook, about how Tyler is making me do everything in the notebook because he's pissed that I posted something about Cooper on Lanesboro Losers. But Kate would definitely want to confront them, and then who knows what they'd do? Besides, this isn't Kate's battle. It's mine.

"No," I say. "It's not about Cooper. It's, uh, it's about something else."

"Okay," she says, still sounding a little worried. "Eliza, I . . ."

But then my cell loses service, and it swallows up the rest

of what she's saying. I click off my phone and slide it into my pocket, not sure what's going to happen next.

After we park the car and start walking toward BU, Marissa starts acting all covert. She's got her cell phone out, and she keeps running her fingers over the buttons.

"What are you doing?" I ask.

"Nothing," she says quickly. "Just checking my voice-mails."

"Okay," I say.

"It doesn't look like you're just checking your voicemails," Clarice points out. "It looks like you're caressing your phone."

"I'm not caressing it," she says. "I just . . ." She sighs. "Do you guys think maybe I should call Jeremiah?"

"Call Jeremiah?" Clarice asks. "Why would you do *that*?"

"Well, because I haven't heard from him since the party," she says.

"If he wanted to talk to you," I say as gently as possible, "then don't you think he would have tried to call you?"

"But there's no reception on the T," she says. "And when I was at the police station, they took my phone. I have no idea if they turned it off or not."

"They didn't turn it off," Clarice says. "And no one called. Trust me."

Clarice looks at me to back her up, but then I decide, you know what? If Marissa wants to call Jeremiah, let her call him. First of all, she's not going to learn anything from us telling her not to do it. The only way she's not going to call him anymore is if she calls him and he's a complete and total jerk to her. The other thing is, I'm a little bit sick of repressing feelings. Why do we have to repress all our feelings? I mean, that's how I ended up with my dumb purple notebook in the first place. I had to actually create a place to write down everything I wanted to do but didn't think I should or could.

"You should call him if you want to," I say, shrugging. Clarice looks at me in shock and opens her mouth like she's going to say something, but then shuts it.

"Thank you, Eliza," Marissa says, shooting Clarice a pointed look. She scrolls through her contact list and then pushes the button for Jeremiah's number. Clarice and I walk a few steps ahead of her, trudging our way down the street and toward Kate's dorm.

"Why did you do that?" Clarice snaps. "You know that nothing good can come of this!"

"Yes, but *she* doesn't know that, and she's not going to know that until she actually calls him and figures it out for herself."

Clarice doesn't look convinced. "We should be looking out for her," she says.

"We can only do so much," I say.

"I know. I got arrested!" Marissa's saying into the phone behind us. "It was crazy. No, I can't really tell you why. It's too much to get into on the phone." I hope she knows that under no circumstances can she tell Jeremiah what went on tonight. I look back at her, and she gives me a look, like "Duh, I'm not going to say anything."

"Okay!" she says happily. "Talk to you then." She ends the call, then does a little twirl in the street, her shadow dancing around under the streetlights. "He's going to call me back," she says. "And when he gets home in a little while, I'm going to go over there." Clarice and I look at each other, and I can tell we're thinking the same thing: booty call. But we don't say it.

When we get to the Perk near Kate's dorm room, a little bit of a fight breaks out. Between the three of us, I mean. Clarice and Marissa have decided they actually want to sit inside of Perk.

"For moral support," Clarice says, and reaches out and rubs my arm.

"Yeah," Marissa says. "For moral support, just in case you chicken out, or if Kate goes mental and decides she wants to kill you or something."

"Thanks," I say. "Those are very comforting scenarios, me chickening out or my sister murdering me. You two are going to be great at giving moral support."

Clarice rolls her eyes. "Of course Kate's not going to go mental and try to kill you," she says, giving me a reassuring smile. But it's the kind of smile your mom gives you when you're about to go into the dentist, and she tells you it's going to be okay, even though you know there's no way it's going to be. "Kate is very classy, she wouldn't freak out in a public place."

Sigh.

"Besides, what are we supposed to do out here?" Marissa asks. "Everything is closed."

"Fine," I say. "But you have to sit all the way back in a corner, and you have to make sure Kate doesn't see you." The last thing I need is my sister getting all excited to see my friends and inviting them to sit with us. She totally would, too. It's one of the reasons everyone loves Kate so much—she's very welcoming.

"Of course," Marissa and Clarice say in unison, and in a certain tone, like of course they wouldn't even think of doing anything to let Kate know they're there.

As I start leaving to head over to Kate's dorm, I hear Clarice say, "Do you think I have to buy another drink here, or does the one I have already count?"

Kate lives on the tenth floor of her building, but I don't even have to buzz her—I run into one of her friends, Cecilia, who signs me in. We ride the elevator up together, with a couple of drunk kids who are laughing and giggling and making the whole place smell like booze and disgustingness. One of the girls keeps going, "Oh my God, you guys, I am REALLY about to throw up, like REALLY," and the rest of them think this is hilariously funny.

When the car stops at the tenth floor, I say goodbye to Cecilia and head down the hall to room 1012. Kate's roommate had this complete breakdown last month and left school, so she has a room to herself. A really small room, but it's still a room to herself.

"Eliza!" Kate yells when she sees me, enveloping me in a huge hug. She's wearing a pair of pink pajama bottoms, and her hair is tied up in a knot. She has on a white T-shirt, and I can see an open textbook on her bed and a cup of tea sitting on her desk.

"Hi," I say, not sure she's going to be so excited to see me when I tell her what I have to tell her.

"Yay! I'm so glad you're here." She jumps up and down, her feet sinking into her fluffy blue throw rug.

"I'm glad I'm here too," I lie.

She sits down on the bed and pats the seat next to her. "Sit," she says.

"So, um, you were studying?" I ask, as I sink down onto the bed next to her. "I'm sorry to interrupt."

"That's okay," she says. She marks her place in her book with a tissue and then slides the book onto the floor and under her bed. I feel very, very guilty. Not just for kissing Miguel, but for interrupting her to tell her such horrible news while she was studying. I mean, Kate *needs* to study. Kate gets really good grades, but she has to work hard. School has never come easily to her, not the way it does to me. "So what's going on, what did you have to tell me?"

Her blue eyes are serious, and I take a deep breath. Suddenly, it feels very hot in here.

"Is it . . . does it feel hot in here to you?" I fan myself with my hand.

"Not really," she says. "But you know I'm always cold. Should I open the window?"

"Yes," I say, and Kate gets up and starts crossing the room.

"Actually," I say, standing up suddenly. "Um, I want to go to Perk."

Kate looks at me like maybe I'm crazy. "O-o-okay," she says slowly. "Are you sure? Because we could have a drink here, I have tea and coffee, and there's a vending machine downstairs if you want something cold."

"I've just really been craving one of those herbal teas they have at Perk," I lie.

"I have herbal tea!" Kate says in delight. "I have tons of—"

"I really want THE KIND THEY HAVE THERE," I say a little too forcefully. "It's organic and caffeine-free." Kate looks taken aback. God, it's hot in here. Seriously, how can she stand it? I feel like maybe I'm going to faint.

"Um, okay," Kate says. She looks at me very strangely and then walks slowly over to her closet. "Let me just get ready."

She pulls a sweatshirt over her head, then changes into jeans and slips her feet into a pair of comfy-looking slides. She redoes her ponytail and then looks at me. "Um, ready?"

"Yes," I say, not so sure. "I'm ready."

We ride the elevator down to the lobby in silence. But I can feel Kate stealing little glances at me out of the corner of her eye. Kind of like she might be really worried about me.

When we get to Perk, I order a peppermint moccaccino, and then lead Kate to a table near the front of the store. The place is pretty empty, actually, and I can see Clarice and Marissa in the back, at a table for four. And to my surprise, the table is full. There are two guys sitting with them who look like college students.

Also, Clarice and Marissa are wearing baseball hats. The guys they're with are bareheaded, and I'm willing to bet that somehow Marissa and Clarice convinced those guys not only to sit with them, but probably to let them wear their hats. Probably for camouflage or something. Unbelievable.

"I thought you wanted an herbal tea," Kate says a little testily once we're settled in at our table.

"What?" I ask. "Oh, yeah, I changed my mind at the last minute."

"You changed your mind? About a drink that you were just dying for a few minutes ago?"

"Yes," I say. I'm too distracted to come up with a plausible excuse, mostly because my eyes are darting around the café, looking for a familiar face. Tyler didn't tell me to sit in a specific seat, so I'm assuming that wherever is fine.

"Eliza, are you okay?" Kate asks. She looks at me with concern.

"I'm fine," I say, plastering a smile onto my face.

"No, I'm serious," she says. "Are you okay? Do you need me to . . . you know, maybe, ah, call someone?"

"Someone like who?" I ask.

"Someone like a therapist or something," she says. "I'm sure we still have Dr. Ronson's number around somewhere."

Dr. Ronson is Kate's old therapist, who she went to see when her best friend Gwen moved away. Kate was thirteen and got so upset about it that she wasn't eating as much as she used to, and my mom got all freaked out and thought maybe Kate was getting an eating disorder. So she sent her to Dr. Ronson, which was kind of ridiculous. Kate saw her for a few months and then seemed to get better. My mom thinks Dr. Ronson's some kind of miracle worker, but honestly I think Kate just needed some time.

"Dr. Ronson?" I ask. "Why would I need to see Dr. Ronson?"

"Because you're acting really weird," she says. "You're all . . . I don't know . . . flustered. I thought you were getting over the whole Cooper thing, you seemed a lot better last time I saw you, but now . . ." She trails off, like she can't believe I'm on such a downslide. If only she knew the half of it.

"Um, no," I say. "I don't need to talk to Dr. Ronson."

"There's no shame in therapy, Eliza," Kate says. "I mean, it helped me." Her saying that breaks the weirdness between us, and we both break into giggles. Kate pretty much thinks Dr. Ronson was full of crap, too, even though, like I said, my mom never stops singing her praises.

I relax a little bit. This is Kate. She's my sister. She loves me. It's going to be okay. But then I look up and see Tyler. He's walking through the door at the other end of the café and is loping toward us, his strides long and easy. He's wearing a pair of jeans and a hunter green pullover. He looks fresh and put together, even though it's after three in the morning.

I guess fucking with people and manipulating them doesn't really do much to tire Tyler out.

For one horrible second, I think Tyler is going to sit down with us. Instead, he takes the seat behind my sister. She can't see him, but I can. He gives me a wink, then pulls a book out of his back pocket and starts to read. Which is so ridiculous, since I've never seen Tyler with a book. Ever. And that includes schoolbooks.

My mouth goes dry. I thought they were going to send someone else, you know, some dumb freshman lackey of theirs who would just spy on my conversation and report back to them. I had no idea it was going to be Tyler himself, staring me down like some kind of . . . snake or something.

"So what is going on, then?" Kate asks. She blows on her coffee. "If you're not upset about Cooper, then what is it?"

"Well," I say. I take a deep breath. "The thing is, I have to tell you something."

"Okay." Kate puts her coffee down, folds her hands in front of her, and waits.

Okay. Deep breath. "Okay, so . . . do you remember Miguel Contador?" And as I'm saying it, I have a wonderful thought: What if she doesn't even *remember* him? Kate's had so many boyfriends since then, maybe he's just totally inconsequential. Maybe she doesn't even *care* about him, maybe now that she's with Brian (her totally perfect and very cute boyfriend who she met over the summer at freshman orientation), she thinks Miguel is just some old high school guy that she can't even remember!

"Of course I remember Miguel Contador," she says. "He was my first love."

I frown. "Miguel was your first love?" Is she serious?

"Yeah," she says.

"But I thought . . . I thought Brian is your first love?"

"No," she says. "I mean, Brian is the first guy I've ever seen myself being with forever," she says. "And I do love him. But Miguel was my first love."

"No," I say, shaking my head.

"No?" Kate repeats, looking confused.

"Yeah, no," I say. "You didn't even like Miguel Contador, don't you remember?"

"No," she says, shrugging. "I mean, yeah, maybe at first I was a little nervous because he was so good-looking." She takes a sip of her coffee. "And I knew he liked me a lot, and I wasn't sure if I really liked him, or if I just liked the idea of him."

But I'm not listening. "What about that guy, you know, um, Dane or whatever? Maybe he was your first love," I say desperately. And I'm not sure if it's my imagination, but I think I see Tyler smirk. What a jerk. I mean, he's not even turning pages. Of his dumb fake book.

"Blane Carver?" Kate asks. "From seventh grade?" She laughs. "No, Eliza, Blane Carver was not my first love."

"But he was your first kiss," I point out.

"Yes, he was my first kiss," she says. "But it was during a game of spin the bottle, and honestly, I didn't even really like him. I just wanted a boyfriend, so when he asked me out later, I said yes."

"Okay," I say morosely.

"Anyway, what about Miguel?" she asks. "Did he . . . he's not dead, is he?"

"Oh God, no; he's not dead," I say. She looks so upset and nervous, like she doesn't know what's coming, but most of all I can tell she's concerned about me, and . . . ugh. This. Is. So. Hard.

It's the only secret I've ever kept from my sister. Ever, ever, ever.

"I need to confess something to you," I say.

"Okay," Kate says. She has her hands folded again, not touching her coffee, and she's looking at me seriously. I take a deep breath and decide to just go for it.

"I . . . I kissed Miguel," I whisper. I don't mean to. Whisper it. But it just . . . I don't know . . . doesn't come out at normal volume.

"What?" Kate asks. "What did you say?"

"I said," I say a little louder this time, "that I kissed him. Uh, Miguel," I clarify just in case she missed it.

"Oh," she says quietly. She takes a small sip of her drink and then regards me across the table. "When?"

"One night," I babble, "when you guys first started going out. It was at that party we had, when Mom and Dad were in San Antonio or something, and we'd gotten ready together beforehand. Me and you had, I mean, not me and Miguel, and you said you weren't sure if you really liked him, and I just . . . I felt jealous." Kate isn't saying anything, she's just looking down into her coffee. "And actually," I keep going, because I don't really know what else to do, "I didn't kiss him, he kissed me, but I . . . I didn't stop him. And I never told you, so in a way, that's even worse than if I had kissed him."

"Why are you telling me this now?" Kate asks, her voice quiet.

"Because I couldn't keep it a secret anymore?" I try.

"Because you couldn't keep it a secret anymore?" Kate repeats.

"I felt guilty," I say. I reach across the table and try to take her hand, but she yanks it away. We sit there for a second, not saying anything. "Say something," I finally say.

"I don't know what to say," she says. She takes a sip of her coffee, then looks at me over the top of her cup. "Tell me," she says, looking me right in the eye, "*exactly* what happened."

So I tell her. Well, as much as I can remember. When I'm finished, she doesn't say anything for a while, just plays with the stir stick in her coffee and stares at the ground.

"Did you ever hook up with him again?" she asks finally, turning her gaze back to me.

"No!" I say, shaking my head vehemently. "No, I *never* hooked up with him again, once I realized you actually liked him, I—"

"Oh," Kate says bitterly. "You didn't hook up with him

after you realized I actually liked him? So when I told you I wasn't sure how I felt about him, *that* was an okay time to kiss him? Even though he was my boyfriend?"

"No," I say again. Tears are filling up my eyes, the same tears that have been threatening to spill for the past hour, only this time they do, running down my cheeks in two salty rivers.

"Eliza, why are you here?" Kate asks, apparently not moved by my tears.

"What do you mean?"

"I mean," she says, her voice getting louder. "That you call me in the middle of the night, you insist we come down here, and then you tell me that you kissed my boyfriend and then kept it a secret for years!"

"*Ex*-boyfriend," I point out. "Not that him being your ex makes it any better, it doesn't, and I'm so so sorry Kate I just—"

"Stop," she says, standing up.

And then she turns on her heel and walks out of Perk. I look up, sure I'm going to see Tyler sitting there with a big smirk on his face. But he's gone. He must have stuck around just long enough to hear me tell Kate, then took off to avoid the fallout.

I pick a napkin up off the table and blow my nose. And then Clarice and Marissa are there, *sans* baseball hats. Their arms are around me and they're hugging me even though I'm a big, sniffling, crying mess.

"What can we do?" Marissa asks.

"I dunno," I say, sniffling. "Can you guys just let me cry for a few minutes?"

"Totally," Clarice says.

And so they do.

Chapter Thirteen

3:57 a.m.

For some reason, I start to think that maybe this is it. That maybe they're all done with me. It's late, I can't imagine anything worse than telling my sister about Miguel, and so after I've cried it out and we're leaving Perk, I've somehow convinced myself that the night will be over soon.

"She's going to forgive you," Clarice says. "I just know it. Y'all are the closest sisters, like, ever. I know it's going to be okay."

"Maybe," I say, taking another sniff. "But maybe not. I mean, what if nothing is the same after this?"

"It *will* be," Clarice says, putting her arm around my shoulders and pulling me close.

"I hope so," I say. We all stand there for a second, not

saying anything. "Well," I say morosely. "I guess the good news is they'll probably give me my notebook back now."

"Why do you think that?" Marissa asks.

"Because," I say. "They just made me do the most horrible thing they could possibly make me do, *and* it's the end of the night."

"Well, that depends on who you're talking to," Marissa says. "It's four in the morning, which to some people is when things are just starting to get going." She pulls out her cell phone and checks the screen, and then I get it. She doesn't want anyone insinuating that the night is over, since Jeremiah still hasn't called her, and so she doesn't know if she's still going over there or not.

"Well, if we're talking about having to do a bunch of things to get your secret notebook back, I would say that four is definitely the cutoff, wouldn't you guys?" I ask.

"I guess so," Clarice says, shrugging. "Hey, where are we going?" We're walking through the streets of Boston kind of aimlessly. The city's pretty dead now. And pretty cold. I shiver and wrap my arms around myself as we walk.

"I don't know," I say. I stop and look around. "I guess we're just going to wait."

"For what?" Clarice asks. "My feet hurt."

"For Tyler to text," I say. "So that he can tell me where to pick my notebook up."

I cross the street without waiting for the sign to change to WALK and jump over the puddles. "When did it rain?" I ask.

"While we were in Perk," Clarice says. "Which is another reason I'm having such a hard time walking. The roads are so slippery." A cab goes flying by, its headlights making rainbows on the pavement.

"Um, Eliza?" Marissa says. "I hate to be the one who says this, but, uh . . . what if they don't give you your notebook back?"

I frown and stop dead in the middle of the sidewalk. Clarice, who's been staring down at her shoes as she walks, slams into my back. I take a step forward, but then luckily catch my balance before I end up falling face-first onto the pavement.

"Why would that happen?" I ask.

"Because I wasn't watching where I was going," Clarice says. "Sorry."

"No, not that," I say. I whirl around and face Marissa. "Why wouldn't they give me my notebook back?"

"We talked about this before, remember?" Marissa says. "Which is why we tried to break into Tyler's and get the notebook?"

"Well, yeah," I say. "But that was before I did all the tasks." A sick feeling is starting in my stomach. It was one thing for me to think about not getting my notebook back at the beginning of the night, before I'd done anything. That was bad enough. But to think about it now, after I've spent all night doing everything they've asked for? That's just unacceptable.

"True," Marissa says. "But they're assholes, Eliza. I wouldn't put it past them."

"No," I say forcefully. "They wouldn't do that." But even as I'm saying it, I don't really believe it. I'm like one of those people on soap operas or nighttime crime dramas who are told their loved ones are dead. They don't believe it, even after they've been told by the doctors and have seen the body.

My phone rings then, in my hand, and I look down at it. Cooper.

I answer it this time. "Hello?" I say angrily. "You better have something good to tell me about how you need to make a time to meet up with me and give me my goddamn notebook back."

Marissa and Clarice look at each other, and a girl walking by us on the street moves around us nervously, giving us a wide berth.

"Eliza," Cooper says, ignoring my snide remark. "Why the fuck haven't you been answering my calls?"

"Oh, I don't know," I say. "Maybe because when I told you I never wanted to speak with you again, I meant it."

"Listen," he says, still ignoring me. "You need to get back to Newton."

"For what?" I ask suspiciously.

"Tyler called a meeting of the 318s at his house, and he's pissed. He knows you guys broke in."

"How does he know we broke in?"

"I guess his parents told him," Cooper reports.

Damn that Mrs. Twill. I knew she was totally untrustworthy. And I should have known there was no way Cal was going to be able to help, he was so completely and totally whipped.

"What jerks," I say.

"Yeah, well, he called a meeting," he says. "Of the 318s. Anyway, I tried to get your notebook back, but it's not there anymore. But I think I have a plan. For how we can get it back."

"What sort of plan?" I ask, even more suspiciously.

"Just . . . meet me outside of Tyler's in half an hour," he says. "Can you do that?" Um, only if we speed and get really, really lucky with traffic and don't get pulled over.

"Yes," I say. "Of course."

"Park down the block," he says. "Where we were before, so that no one sees you."

And then he hangs up before I have a chance to ask him any more questions or protest or anything!

"What did he say?" Clarice asks.

"He said to meet him outside of Tyler's in half an hour," I say. "He says he has a plan to get the notebook back."

"And you believe him?" Marissa asks.

"I'm not sure," I say. But the truth is, I kind of do. Cooper hasn't really lied to me about anything tonight. He's helped me, even though at points I was a total and complete bitch to him. Of course, that could all be part of the master plan, where he and the 318s try to lull me into a false sense of security, only to let the whole thing come crashing down on me later, when I do decide to trust them at the worst possible moment. Cooper could totally be like the boy who cried *wolf*; only it's the boy who cried *notebook*. And in reverse, since I would believe him at the end instead of not believing him. Whatever.

"So what are you going to do?" Clarice asks. I hesitate. On one hand, I really do not want to rely on Cooper for anything, and part of me wants to just wait it out. Maybe the 318s are having a meeting so that they can figure out a way to get me my notebook back. Maybe they're going to make me do a couple of other things, but in the end will stick to their part of the bargain. Maybe I should just give it a little more time.

My phone goes off with a text then, and I look down at the screen. Tyler. "LAST TASK," it says. "COME TO MY HOUSE SO THAT YOU CAN TELL COOPER HOW YOU REALLY FEEL ABOUT HIM."

Well. That settles that.

In my defense, I'd totally had some wine. When I wrote it, I mean. The stuff in my notebook about Cooper and how I really feel about him. I mean how I *felt* about him. It was a few days after we broke up, and I got super-upset and spent all afternoon crying in my room.

Later that night, I called Kate, and she rode the T all the way in from Boston and then took me back to her dorm. I skipped school the next day and, instead, Kate and I spent the day eating. We went from restaurant to restaurant, bakery to bakery, store to store. We bought hamburgers and cupcakes and ice cream. If we couldn't decide between flavors or entrées, we got them both and wrapped up the leftovers.

By the time the day was over, we had sore stomachs but, somehow, I felt better. We took the T back to our house and sat on the deck, drinking wine and watching the sun set. Kate was working on a project for school, and I had my notebook out, scribbling away as the sun dipped down and threatened to leave me with not enough light to complete my thoughts.

For the first time, I wrote almost more of a diary entry. My purple notebook, up until that point, had been a list of things I wanted to do but was scared of. It was disjointed with cross outs all over the place and sentences scratched in my seventh-grade self's handwriting. Names of boys and friends I no longer knew littered the pages.

But this time, I felt like I needed to write something more. Something about Cooper. I wrote that if I was really being honest, that I wouldn't have just screamed at Cooper and stomped out of his house that day. If I was really being honest, I thought that maybe I was falling in love with Cooper, and that maybe, if he apologized, I would take him back. I said that I wished I could talk to him, that I wished I could find out how much of what he had showed me over the past couple of months had been fake and how much hadn't been. I wrote about how he was deeper than everyone thought, and how I really needed to know what part of him was true.

Honestly, it was very overdramatic, very pathetic, and definitely embarrassing. And I'm sure that's the part Tyler is hoping I'm going to read. He's obviously setting up this big meeting at his house so that I'll have to do it there, in front of everyone.

Which is, you know, not an option.

Which is why Cooper is my last hope and why I'm rushing Clarice and Marissa back to Newton before anything horrible happens.

But by the time we get the car and get on the road, I'm starting to think that we're not going to make it.

"We're not going to make it," I say to Marissa. "I just know it."

Clarice is in the backseat, on the phone with Jamie, who seems to be talking about how she can't believe how close she came to being involved in a drive-by or something tonight. Which is totally ridiculous and very annoying.

"I'm going as fast as I can," Marissa says. "I swear."

"I know you are," I say, watching as the speedometer inches close to eighty. My life pretty much depends on us getting back to Newton in time to meet up with Cooper, but still. I don't want Marissa going any faster, since as bad as tonight has been, I really would prefer to stay alive. Not to mention if we get pulled over, it's definitely going to put a crimp in our night, and I will have no car and no way to get anywhere. I grip the sides of my seat and decide to look on the bright side—at least Marissa hasn't been drinking.

"Maybe you should call Cooper," Marissa says.

"Call Cooper?" I frown. "For what?"

"To tell him we might be a little late," Marissa says. "Maybe he can delay the meeting or something."

"Yeah," I say. But I really, really do not want to do that. Calling Cooper means that I need him, that I'm actually dependent on his help. And even if that's true, I don't want him to know that. Otherwise, he'll be able to . . . well . . . I don't know what he'll be able to do, but I just don't want him to know.

"I'm just saying," she says. "It might be better."

"Fine," I say, sighing. I pull out my phone and scroll through until I find Cooper's number. I take a deep breath and then push the button.

"Hey," he says when he answers.

I swallow. "Hey," I say. "It's me. It's Eliza." I clarify, just in case.

"Where are you?" he says. "I have to go into the meeting soon."

"We're almost there," I say. "Can you stall them just ten more minutes?"

"I'll try," he says. But he doesn't sound so sure.

"What did he say?" Marissa asks.

"He said he would try," I say. I slide my phone into my bag and lean my head back against the seat. There's nothing to do now except watch the highway fly by and cross my fingers that we get there on time.

When we pull off the highway, I call Cooper again. I don't know why—I guess to give him an update. This is why I didn't want to call Cooper in the first place. Once you break the seal on something like that, everything just breaks wide open. I mean, look at me, calling Cooper left and right now.

"Hey," I say. "We're almost there."

"Okay," he says. "I'm parked down the street, and I'm supposed to be at Tyler's, like, now, so I won't have too much time to talk."

"Okay." I say slowly. Why does he want to talk? What do we need to talk about? If he has my notebook, then can't he just give it to me? I want to ask him, but I also don't want to tip him off in case this whole thing is a big setup.

So I just hang up.

When we pull onto Tyler's street, Cooper's parked where he said he would be. We pull up behind him, and he runs out of the car and over to the passenger-side door. I roll the window down.

"Hey." He looks around furtively, maybe because he doesn't want to get caught, but maybe because he's waiting for backup.

"Where is it?" I demand. "Do you have it? Or at least some kind of plan?" I roll the window down a little so that it's just slightly cracked.

"I couldn't get the notebook," he says.

"You couldn't?" I repeat, my heart sinking.

"No," he says. "Tyler moved it, and I don't know to where. But I have something even better." And then he slides something through the window to me, a really thin black notebook with a leather cover. From behind us comes the sound of a car driving down the street, and Cooper looks behind him and then says, "I gotta go."

He runs back to his car, and then he's gone.

"What the fuck?" Marissa asks. She reaches over and pulls the black notebook off my lap. "What is this?"

I snatch it back from her and open it up.

The first page says, "The Order of the 318s, Official Documents and Procedures." The second page looks like some kind of oath or creed. It's typed up in a cursive font, very official and sort of old-looking. But more like it's trying to look old, not like it really is.

"We, the undersigned, pledge our undying loyalty to the order of the 318s." There are hundreds of signatures filling the pages following.

I page through. And then it dawns on me. Cooper has given me some kind of pledge book, some kind of secret notebook of the 318s.

"Oh my God," I say.

"What is it?" Clarice asks, off the phone now. "What was Cooper saying? I missed the whole thing."

"He said he couldn't get her notebook back and then he dropped that thing on Eliza's lap," Marissa reports.

"What is it?" Clarice asks. She pushes her head between the two seats.

"It's *their* notebook," I say. "It's . . . it's everything about the 318s, including all their members."

"Oh. My. God." Marissa looks at me in awe.

"We could totally give that to the school," Clarice says. And she's right. The school is always trying to figure out who the 318s are, especially when they do their "anonymous" pranks.

It's all here in front of me. Their names. Their signatures. Lists of the pranks they've done. Their dumb oaths and their dumb rituals and even lists of things they're considering doing.

"You can do *anything* with that," Marissa says. "You could use it to get them to drop your disciplinary hearing."

"And," I say, "I can trade it for *my* notebook." I run my hand over the first page.

"Cooper is going to get into a lot of trouble for giving that to you," Clarice says. She claps her hands. "He must really care about you, Eliza."

"Yeah," I say. "Or he just feels guilty for being a complete and total prick, and now he wants to do something to make himself feel better."

"That's a pretty big thing to do just to make yourself feel better," Clarice says. She settles back into her seat.

"So what do we do now?" Marissa asks.

"Now," I say. "We go to Kinko's."

Chapter Fourteen

5:21 a.m.

We have to drive twenty minutes to find a Kinko's that's open twenty-four hours, so we plug the address into the GPS, crank the music, and roll down the windows. I let the brisk early morning air fly through my hair, and then I push all thoughts of this horrible night out of my mind for a little while. It feels SO. GOOD.

When we get to Kinko's, we spend half an hour photocopying the 318s' notebook onto sparkly purple paper, which we then take and put into a glittery pink binder with a butterfly on it. The guy at Kinko's thinks we're kind of crazy, but I'm really having too much fun to care.

"Smiley-face stickers?" Marissa suggests, taking a package of them off a rack and holding them up.

"Are they pink?" I ask.

"No." She puts them back on the rack. "Ooh, ballet slippers!" she says. She pulls open the package and starts to decorate the spine of the binder.

The guy working there gives us a nervous look from his place behind the counter. Probably he's never seen a bunch of girls coming in with a secret society's confidential binder that they're making a copy of.

Clarice taps her long fingernails on the side of a copy machine. "Explain to me again why we're photocopying this?" she says. "I mean, we already have the notebook."

"Yes," I say, affixing a tutu sticker to the cover of the binder as a final touch. "But now we have a copy."

"So?" She stares at me blankly.

"So now we can trade their notebook for mine, but we have *this* copy"—I hold up the pink monstrosity—"as backup in case they ever decide to start their crap again."

"Oh." Clarice looks like I've just taken away her innocence. "Kind of like . . . *extortion*," she whispers.

"Well, not really," I say. "More like blackmail. But they started it."

Marissa nods. "Okay," she says. "Now what should we—"

Her phone starts ringing then, and she looks at the caller ID. "Jeremiah," she whispers. "I almost . . . I mean, I kind of forgot about him." She looks dazed, like she can't really imagine that she could ever forget about Jeremiah. She flips open her phone and steps away for a second, over near a big table that's piled high with office supplies.

I gather up all the stuff we've used, bring it over to the cash register, and drop it down on the counter.

The guy who works there looks down and sighs.

"Sorry, Sam," I say, reading his name tag and surveying the jumble of empty packages, ripped-open stickers, cellophane, and, of course, the pinkalicious binder. "I guess I kind of made a mess."

"Kind of?" he asks. But not in an unfriendly way. In more of an, "Oh, God, how am I going to deal with this?" kind of way.

"If you knew the night I've had," I say, "you would understand."

He gives me a thin smile, then picks up the binder and scans it.

From behind me, I can hear Marissa on the phone. "Yeah," she's saying. "I'm glad you had fun. No, I know, I just . . . I'm not . . ."

I start to feel a little nervous as I realize what's going on. Jeremiah is finally calling Marissa, but it's way too late to hang out. He probably spent the night getting drunk and grinding on different girls, and now he's giving her some dumb excuse for why he didn't call. I'm pissed, not only because I don't want Marissa to get hurt, but because the three of us are having so much fun. And now Jeremiah's going to put her in a bad mood and ruin everything.

I look at Clarice, who is using one of the plate-glass floor-to-ceiling windows to check her reflection and give herself the once-over. She turns around, and I can tell we're thinking the same thing. Whatever Jeremiah's telling Marissa is complete and total bullshit.

Sam the cashier finishes ringing up my ballet stickers. "Your total is seventy-six dollars and eighteen cents," he announces.

But I'm not really paying attention. I'm still trying to spy on Marissa's conversation. "Yeah," she's saying. "It's fine, I can probably come over later today instead. I just don't understand why you didn't call me earlier." Marissa just listens for a minute. And then, it's like a switch flips. And Marissa starts to, um, go a little crazy. "You were SMOKING UP with Brendan and Robbie?" she yells. Her eyes get really wide and start to bug out of her head. "And you had to hang out with them because I LOST YOUR POT? I did not *lose* it, Jeremiah; I got it TAKEN FROM ME BY THE POLICE."

Sam the cashier looks at me nervously, and I try to give him a reassuring smile. I'm about to tell him it was a total misunderstanding, that Marissa's not a druggie or a dealer or anything, but Marissa's still practically screaming. "You know, actually, I don't think I *will* be coming over later. I'm busy." And then she ends the call. I look at her. She looks at me. Clarice looks at her. She looks at Clarice. Me and Clarice look at each other, and then we both look back at Marissa.

"*Jeremiah*," she says, "couldn't call me earlier because he was getting high with his dumb friends. And apparently he thinks it's my fault since I lost his pot. He invited me over later today, but I said I was busy." She looks shocked at her own behavior, like she can't believe for the life of her that she would say something like that.

"Good for you," I say.

"*Great* for you," Clarice says.

"Is someone going to pay me?" Sam asks.

When we get outside, I have three messages from Tyler, and judging from his tone, he doesn't seem too happy.

Message one: "All right, why the fuck aren't you answering? You have five minutes to call me back, otherwise I'm putting your notebook up on the web. I don't even care."

He's bluffing, of course, because I have two other messages from him. I'm glad I didn't get that first one, because I might have just been scared enough to call him back.

Message two: "Fine, Eliza. Look, I'm sorry we did this. We were mad, okay? You tried to mess with us and bring us down." Actually, I didn't. What I did was post something that was very true (okay, halfway true) online about one of their members. But whatever. Semantics, I guess. "Just give us back our notebook, and we'll give you back yours, and we can just forget the whole thing ever happened."

And then, finally, the third message, where Tyler has somehow turned into some kind of whiny thirteen-year-old.

Message three: "Eliza, please, can you just give it back to us? We don't care what you post on Lanesboro Losers, we just really need that notebook back."

I put the phone on speaker and play back all the messages for Marissa and Clarice.

"Wow," Clarice says. "He's, like, desperate."

"He's probably going to get his ass kicked," Marissa says. We're sitting in the car, the notebook and the pinkalicious binder sitting on the front seat. We stopped at the twenty-four-hour Walgreens next door to Kinko's, where we bought snacks. And now we're gorging ourselves while listening to the messages.

"Who would kick his ass?" I ask, taking a drink of my Snapple.

"The big boss," Marissa says.

"Ooh, like in the mob!" Clarice says. She nods wisely, as if she knows all about organized crime. She leans over the seat and says, "Do we have any napkins up there?"

Marissa points to the glove compartment, and I pop it open and hand Clarice some napkins.

"Thank you," she says, and wipes her hands daintily.

"What do you mean, 'the big boss'?" I ask.

"Well, the 318s have been around for years," Marissa says. "I'm sure they have some kind of leader, some kind of guy who's the one in charge."

"Tyler's in charge," I say, taking a big handful of caramel corn and popping it into my mouth. "Isn't he?"

"He's the president," Marissa says. "But there's probably someone else, like someone who's been around for a while who, like, heads up the organization. Probably some forty-year-old fat, balding man who is way too invested in what the 318s are doing and wants to live his glory days over and over through them."

"Hmm," I say, considering this.

"That's what they do in my dad's old college frat," Marissa says. "They even have these dumb reunions where they get together every year and rent a party bus. Then they get drunk and ogle college girls and pretend they have a chance with them."

"Wow," I say.

"Wow," Clarice says.

"Totally," Marissa says, nodding. "So are you going to call him back so we can make the exchange?"

"Yeah," I say, sighing. "I should probably call him back." As much as I enjoy letting Tyler sweat it out, I do want my notebook back. And that will necessitate calling him back to meet up.

But when I pull my phone out, it rings in my hand. Cooper.

"Hello?" I say.

"Eliza?" he says. No *hey* this time.

"Yeah?" I say.

"Look, we want our notebook back."

"No, I know," I say. "I was just making a copy of it, it was —"

"Can you meet us in the school parking lot? In fifteen minutes?" He cuts me off, and then I get it. Tyler's with him. They probably figured that if Cooper called me, I'd answer. Which means they think I'm still half in love with him, which really pisses me off, since (a) I'm not and (b) the only reason I even answered the dumb phone was because I was about to call Tyler anyway.

"Yes," I say. "I'll meet you there." And then I hang up on him just in case he thinks I only answered because it was him.

When we get to the school, the parking lot is empty.

"Where exactly did they say?" Marissa asks.

"I dunno," I say. "They just said the parking lot."

"This place is really spooky," Clarice says. Her eyes are wide as she looks out the window and takes it all in. The thing is, she's right. This place *is* kind of spooky. The sun is just starting to peek up over the horizon, but for the most part, it's still dark out. And even though there are lights in the parking lot, every space is empty, which just seems . . . wrong. Even when school's out, the parking lot's never empty, since there are always after-school activities or dances or sporting events or *something* going on.

"I really wish we wouldn't have gotten here first," I say. "It's like getting somewhere first before a blind date—it's awkward."

"You've never been on a blind date," Marissa points out.

"Yes, but I've seen tons of movies with blind dates in them," I say. "Which is almost the same."

We circle around the school a few times and then finally park over by the side of the gym. I lean my head back on the seat and look up at the streetlights. A bunch of moths are flying around, attracted by the light, and I watch them for a second. The only sounds are the radio playing really softly in the car, and the heater blowing warm air out on its lowest setting.

Now that the high of getting the 318s' notebook has faded, the whole thing with Kate is at the forefront of my mind, and it won't go away. I mean, yeah, it's been there kind of the whole time, nagging me, but I think I was using getting my notebook back as a distraction, and now that the distraction is gone, I can't stop thinking about it. I pull my phone out and text Kate. "LOVE YOU K. AND I AM SO SO SORRY."

Five minutes later, she still hasn't texted me back.

Ten minutes later, she still hasn't texted me back, *and* Tyler still hasn't shown up. So I start to freak out.

"What if they're not coming?" I ask.

"They're coming," Marissa says.

"But what if they don't?"

"Then you turn the bastards' notebook in to the school," Clarice says vengefully from the backseat.

"But what if it doesn't work?" I ask. "What if it was some kind of decoy notebook? What if it's not even real? What if they don't even care that I have their notebook? What if they just decided that they would post mine, anyway?"

"You think they made up a whole notebook just to fool you?" Marissa asks doubtfully.

"They're not smart enough for that," Clarice pipes up helpfully.

"But what if—"

I don't get a chance to finish, though, because at that moment the sound of car engines fills the air. Driving toward us are three cars, all of them filled with guys.

"Oh my God," I say. "They brought their whole . . . their whole . . . *posse*."

"Posse?" Clarice repeats. She wrinkles her tiny nose. "I don't think anyone says *posse* anymore." She reaches into her purse and pulls out what looks like a small can of hair spray. "But don't worry, I have pepper spray."

"Pepper spray?" I ask.

"Yeah, you know, if they try to do anything." She shrugs. "You can't be too careful, Eliza. You should have some too, the way you gallivant around the city all by yourself."

"What do you mean?" I frown. "Tonight is the first time I've ever 'gallivanted' around the city by myself, and it doesn't really count because not only did I not have a choice, I definitely didn't have time to stop at a store and pick up any kind of self-defense paraphernalia. And besides—"

"Anyway," Marissa says, holding up her hand and cutting me off. "They're not going to hurt us." She opens her door and steps out of the car. "They're just pretending to be all macho."

"How do you know?" I ask, looking at the car door handle and wondering if I should lock the door and stay in the car, or risk it and get out.

"Because there are cameras all over this parking lot," she

says. "Remember last year when Tyler got busted for graffiti? He knows there are cameras, do you really think he's going to hurt us?"

"What if they're wearing masks?" I ask. "So that no one will be able to tell who they are?"

"The cameras would pick up their cars," Marissa says. She puts her hands on her hips. She's out of the car now, and she looks at me through the open door.

"What if they take us to an undisclosed location?" I ask. "With no cameras?"

"How would they do that if we refuse to get in the car?"

"I dunno," I say.

"I'm still bringing my pepper spray," Clarice declares. She loops the keychain part of it around her finger.

We both reluctantly get out of the car and walk around behind it. The parking lot is actually lit really well, which makes me feel a little bit better.

Tyler gets out of his car, and for a second, I feel like we're going to have some kind of showdown or, like, shoot-out or something. A few more guys get out of the cars around him, including Cooper. I avert my eyes and look down at the ground.

"Did you bring it?" Tyler asks. In his hand is my purple notebook.

"Yeah, I brought it," I say. I pull his black notebook out from behind my back and show it to him.

He holds his hand out.

"No way," I say, pulling it back. "You first." If he thinks he's going to get me to give him his notebook first, he's crazy.

"No," he says. "You first." I narrow my eyes.

"*You* first." This is ridiculous.

"Fine." Tyler holds the notebook out and I move toward him, but at the last second, he yanks it back.

"Real mature," I say. I mean, really.

"Who gave you our pledge book?" he asks.

"What do you mean?" I ask, trying to play innocent.

"Who," he says, a little more growly this time, "gave you the 318s' charter?"

"No one *gave* it to me," I say. "I broke into your house and stole it."

"No, you didn't," Tyler says. "My parents said you didn't have anything when you left, and I was there after you were. The notebook was still there, and then it was gone."

"Yeah, well." I shrug and give him a smile. "So are you ready to make the exchange?"

"No," Tyler says. "I want you to tell me who gave you that notebook." And then I realize this is my chance. My chance to really get back at Cooper. If I tell on him, if I let Tyler know Cooper was the one who gave me the notebook, who knows what Tyler would do? He would definitely set out to make Cooper's life a living hell.

It wouldn't even be that hard. For me, I mean. All I'd have to do is say his name, and I could totally get him back. But unfortunately, as much as I don't want to admit it, I still care about Cooper. And I'd feel horrible for turning on him after he risked his own ass for me. Besides, it doesn't matter. As long as I get my notebook back, getting the 318s to go after Cooper serves no real purpose.

"Yeah, well, I'm not going to tell you," I say finally, being careful not to look across the parking lot at Cooper.

Tyler turns around then and looks at all of the 318s who are gathered around him. "I want to know," he says. "Who gave her the notebook? And why did you do it?" And then I realize that's why he brought everyone here. Not so he could hurt me or yell at me or outnumber me. He brought everyone here so that he could try to figure out who gave me the notebook. He looks around at all of the 318s and holds the gaze of each one. Honestly, it's a little bit ridiculous. I mean, could they be any more full of themselves? Lame.

When Tyler gets to Cooper, Cooper holds his gaze steady. For a second, my heart leaps into my chest, and I wonder if maybe Cooper might say something himself. If he might admit that he's the one who gave me the notebook, if he might stick up for me, if he might tell the 318s that what they did to me was wrong.

But he doesn't say anything, and Tyler just moves on to try and intimidate the next person. I swallow my disappointment. Whatever. I mean, if he wanted to say something, he would have done it before now. I've totally been watching too many romantic comedies where, at the end of the movie, the guy makes some big grand declaration before the couple ends up happy and walks off into the sunset. Or in this case, I guess we'd walk off into the sunrise.

Anyway.

"Look," I say, my grip tightening on the notebook. "While it's nice for you to bring everyone here and show off your intimidation tactics, I'd like to get home. It's been kind of a long night, if you know what I mean."

"Whatever," Tyler says.

I take a couple of steps toward him, and he takes a couple of steps toward me. I give him the black notebook, and he gives me mine at exactly the same time. Our hands touch for a moment, and a shiver goes through me. And not in a good way.

"Oh," I say, as I make my way back toward the car, my notebook safely in my hand. "Just fyi, I made a copy of your pledge book." Tyler's jaw drops. "Don't worry, I'm not going to do anything with it, but I trust you're going to drop the complaint you filed with the dean about what I posted on Lanesboro Losers."

Tyler's mouth tightens into a line. "Fine," he says.

"Thanks," I say sweetly. "I *so* totally appreciate it." And then I turn around and head back to the car. Marissa and Clarice follow me, and we all climb in.

Right before she shuts the door, Clarice looks behind her at the 318s, who are standing in the parking lot, looking a little stunned and dejected.

"You're lucky," she yells at them, "that I didn't have to use my pepper spray."

She slams the door, and Marissa peels out of the parking lot.

Chapter Fifteen

6:47 a.m.

We go to a diner to celebrate.

The sun is really coming up now, and it's turning the sky shades of pink and purple and blue and warming up the air. It's a welcome sight after such a long night, and suddenly, even though we just had snacks not that long ago, I'm famished.

"I want pancakes," I decide once we're settled in the booth, and when the waitress comes around, that's just what I get. A big stack of pancakes with chocolate chips and whipped cream and then to top it off, I pour syrup over the whole thing. After the night I've had, I deserve it. And honestly, who cares? I don't eat like this all the time, but I also don't care to look like a stick figure. I pour an extra glob of syrup on for good measure.

"Oh my God," Clarice says, shoving her phone at us across the table. "Are you kidding me? Look at what Jamie's last Facebook update says!"

I squint at the screen.

"It says, 'watching a movie with my bestie,'" Clarice scoffs and looks at me and Marissa, waiting for a reaction.

"What's wrong with that?" Marissa asks. She takes a sip of her soda.

"Yeah," I say. "What's wrong with that? It sounds nice." It totally does, too. This night is making it feel like it's been at least five years since we just stayed in and watched a movie.

"The problem *is*," Clarice says, "that her bestie is her sister, Madeline, who is the one who left her in Southie tonight!"

"So they made up," I say. "Like sisters do." I swallow and think of Kate, then check my phone again for the thousandth time. Still no text.

"They made up," Clarice says, "two hours after she left her in the ghetto!"

"It wasn't exactly the ghetto," I point out. "And nothing bad happened to her."

Clarice looks down at her phone forlornly, like if she stares at it enough, the Facebook status will change.

But Marissa notices the look on my face, and she reaches over and squeezes my hand. "Hey," she says. "You and Kate are going to be fine."

"How do you know?" I ask.

"Because Kate loves you," Clarice says. "Of course she's going to forgive you."

"I never should have told her," I say, spearing a piece of pancake and chewing on it thoughtfully. "She never would have found out."

"Eliza!" Clarice says. "That's not true! You needed to tell her, otherwise you would have always had a secret from her, which would have totally marred your sisterhood!"

"She's right," Marissa says. "Now you guys can deal with it and get over it."

"Hopefully," I say, checking my phone again even though it's only been two seconds.

"She probably went to sleep," Marissa says, seeing me check my phone.

"Yeah," I say, forcing a smile. "You're probably right."

There's silence for a little bit as we all chew our food and sip our drinks. Then Clarice picks her phone back up. "New e-mail alert," she says. "'One of your friends has posted new pictures on Lanesboro Losers.' I wonder who—Eliza! You posted new pics?"

"What?" I ask, confused. "No, I haven't." And then I remember. Cooper. The camera. Me. In a bathing suit. "Oh my God," I say, reaching across the table and trying to grab the phone out of her hand before she can see it. But it's too late.

"Wow," she says, her eyes widening.

"I'm deleting it," I say.

"What picture is it?" Marissa asks.

"It's the picture Cooper took of me," I say.

Clarice passes the phone to Marissa. "Wow," she says. "You look hot."

I look at the picture on the phone, even though I already saw it earlier. "You know what?" I say. "I think maybe I might leave it up."

After our carb-laden breakfast, I crash. Hard. The adrenaline that's been coursing through my veins all night is gone, my coffee wore off hours ago, and all the sugar and whipped cream is making me sluggish and sleepy.

"Are you guys still staying over?" I ask as Marissa pulls her car onto my street.

"I have to go home," Marissa says. "Grounded, remember? I have to sneak back in."

"Oh, right," I say, shaking my head. "I forgot you were arrested tonight, that's so weird."

"I'm going to go home too," Clarice says. "I have to get up early tomorrow. I mean, today. Me and Jamie are going to play tennis."

"You guys," I say, looking at them both. I think about how they stood by my side tonight, how they were there for me, how they stuck by me and helped me through what's probably been the hardest night of my life. "Thanks for tonight. For everything."

"You're welcome," Marissa says.

"What are friends for?" Clarice adds with a smile.

I open the car door and make my way to my front porch. I'm so tired I can barely walk up the steps, and all I can think about is how good my bed is going to feel, how amazing it's going to be to get out of these clothes and into a nice comfy pair of pajama pants and a tank top. I'm sliding my key into the lock when the sound of a car pulling into the driveway interrupts my thoughts of clean, crisp sheets and a warm, cozy bed.

I turn around and see a red BMW. Cooper.

"Hey," he says, getting out of the car and walking up my driveway.

"Hey," I say. The sun is completely over the horizon now, and it's that perfect time of the morning, when it's still sunny and bright, and you can almost trick yourself into thinking it's going to warm up and be a nice day.

Cooper walks up onto the porch and kicks the toe of his shoe against the concrete.

"Oh my God," I say. "What happened to your face?" Cooper has a reddish bruise under his eye, and it looks all shiny and a little bit swollen. I resist the urge to reach out and run my finger over it, to make sure he's okay.

"Nothing," he says. I give him a skeptical look, and he sighs. "Fine, Tyler found out I was the one who gave you our pledge book and let's just say he wasn't too pleased."

"You guys got into a fight?" I ask.

"Not really," he says. "It was more like a . . . a little scrape." He looks away and I reach out and grab his chin, moving his face back so I can get a better look at the bruise. His skin feels warm and all scruffy under my fingers. "It's fine," he says. "The guys broke it up before it could really escalate."

"Ouch," I say. I pull my hand away from his face, and my fingers feel like they're on fire. "I didn't tell him. That you were the one who gave it to me."

"I know," he says. "I was there, remember?" But he doesn't say it in a cocky way.

"So then how did he find out?"

"I told him." He's staring at me now, his eyes searching mine.

"Oh." I swallow. "Are you . . . did you . . . Why did you tell him?"

"Because I didn't want anything to do with them anymore," he says. "After what they did to you tonight. The only reason I didn't stop it before is because I knew they would have made it even worse for you."

"Thanks," I say truthfully. "You helped me a lot tonight."

"You're welcome," he says. He starts to say something else, but I cut him off.

"I have to go in now," I say.

"Oh," he says. "Are you sure?"

"Yeah," I say. I put my hand back on my key, which is still in the lock, and Cooper turns away and starts to walk down the driveway, and I think about how lucky I am that I didn't have to tell him what I wrote about him in my notebook. And then my heart skips a beat. Because I wonder what would happen if I *did* tell him, if I stopped pretending that I didn't care, if I just told him how I really felt.

"Hey," I say, turning back around. "Why'd you do it?"

"Do what?" he asks.

"Ask me out," I say. "Put my name on that list."

"I don't know," he says, walking back toward the porch. "I didn't . . . I didn't want to. I just . . . I wasn't looking at it the same way they were."

"What do you mean?" I ask.

"They thought it would be fun to mess with some girls, to get them to believe they were really interested in them. . . . And I . . ." He trails off and then shoves his hands into his pockets, looking down at the ground. When he looks back up at me, he says, "One time last year I saw you outside at lunch. You were reading something in your history book, and drinking a juice box, and you were wearing an iPod and a pink hoodie, and your lips were moving but no sound was coming out, and ever since then I wanted to talk to you."

"If that's true," I say, "then why didn't you?"

"Chicken," he says. "I thought you were too smart for me."

"You're right," I say. "I am too smart for you."

He laughs. "Eliza," he says, and takes a step closer. "I swear to God, I didn't want to hurt you. After the first day, I completely forgot about the real reason I asked you out."

"You could have told me," I say.

"I know." He's really close now, and my heart is beating so fast and my stomach feels all crazy and wobbly. "I'm sorry."

I take a deep breath and think about what I wrote about

him in my notebook, about how badly he hurt me, about how much he made me cry. "You really, really hurt me," I say. "I liked you so much, Cooper. I liked you so, so much."

"I liked you, too, so, so much," he says. "Can you . . . could you ever think about forgiving me?"

He's so close now, and I can smell his laundry soap and the cologne I gave him and see where his sideburns fade into the sides of his face. His eyes are searching mine, and I open my mouth to say something, to give in, to tell him yes, not because I'm a sucker, but because I believe him, because he helped me tonight, because I think he's telling the truth. But before I can say anything, his lips are on mine, and we're kissing and it feels right and good and exactly the way things are supposed to be.

"You do know you're in a lot of trouble with me," I say, when we finally pull apart.

"I know," he says into my hair.

"And you know that you're going to have to spend days and days and months and months making it up to me before I forgive you?"

"I'll do it," he says. "I'll watch hours and hours of cheesy eighties movies with you."

"Do you promise?" I ask.

"Promise," he says. And then he kisses me again.

Later, after I make Cooper leave (Um, hello! Yeah, I'm giving him another chance, but the boy has to grovel and work for my attention at least a little bit—plus, you know, I'm pretty exhausted) and we make plans to talk later that day, I head out onto the back deck with my notebook.

And I read the whole thing, cover to cover. My seventh-grade fears. My eighth-grade fears. Every single thing I've ever been afraid to do, right here in one book. I realize I did some of them tonight, and nothing horrible happened. I didn't die. In fact, I learned a lot about myself and about the things I'm capable of doing. I realized that my friends are true. And that sometimes people make mistakes and deserve second chances.

I sit there on the lounge chair for a second after I'm done. The sun is completely up now, and the next door neighbors are in their driveway, getting ready to go to church. The birds are chirping, and the day's getting warmer.

I pick up my notebook, and bring it over to the corner of our deck, where the fire pit is. Then I pick up the box of matches that we have out there, light one, and drop it onto the pages.

I wrap my arms around myself and watch for a few minutes, while everything I'm afraid of goes up in flames, turning into shades of red and orange and yellow and blue. I watch it for a long time, thinking about the night, about Cooper, about how everything can change so drastically in such a short period of time. My phone vibrates in my pocket, and I pull it out. One new text. "LOVE YOU TOO E," it says. "TALK TMR XXXO, K." I smile and slide the phone back into my pocket. And finally, when my notebook's nothing but ashes, I put the fire out and head up to bed.

Ready for more?
Turn the page for a sneak peek at
Sometimes It Happens,
also by Lauren Barnholdt

The First Day of Senior Year

I really should *not* be so scared. I mean, I've done this millions of times before. Okay, maybe not millions. But for the last twelve years, on every weekday minus summers and vacations, I've gone to school. And I've never been afraid before. (Well, except for maybe a little bit in kindergarten, but isn't everyone a little afraid in kindergarten? And besides, even then I wasn't freaking out or anything. Not like Layna Hodge, who threw up all over the play box in the corner.)

Today, the first day of senior year, I'm terrified. This is because there is a very good chance that at some point today I will:

a. lose the love of my life,

b. lose my best friend, or

c. have an awkward encounter with the boy who broke my heart last year. (Note: This is a different boy than the previously mentioned love of my life. [See a.])

I take a deep breath and grip the steering wheel of my new car, then pull into a spot in the visitor lot of my high school. I'm technically not supposed to be parked here, but the visitor lot is way closer to my homeroom than the student lot, and since it's the first day of school, I'm pretty sure I can get away with it. Plus it won't be as obvious if I have to peel out of here and make an escape. *Okay*, I tell myself, *you can do this. You are invincible; nothing can rattle you. You have nerves of steel; you are a confident, strong woman; you—*

There's a knock on the passenger side window and I scream, then immediately hit the automatic door locks.

I look over. Oh. It's only Lacey.

She knocks on the window again, and I reluctantly unlock the doors.

She slides into the passenger seat, her long, red curly hair pooling around her shoulders. She smells like coffee and strawberry-mango shampoo.

"Hey," she says. "What's wrong? Why'd you freak out when I knocked on your window? And why are you parked in the visitor lot? It took me forever to find you."

"Nothing's wrong," I say. Which is a lie, of course. But I can't tell Lacey that. She knows nothing about what went on this summer. She knows nothing of the fact that my best friend Ava is coming back today, that everything is different, and that everything is horrible. That I'm going to see Noah, that I'm going to see Sebastian, that I'm going to maybe end up in a mental institution by the end of the day. Although, a mental institution actually might be preferable to going to school, so that might not be such a bad thing, now that I think about it.

"Just normal first day of school nerves," I say brightly.

"First day of school nerves?" Lacey says, like she's never heard of them. Which kind of makes no sense, since Lacey is one of the most nervous people I know. "You need caffeine then," she says. "It will fix you right up." She holds out the cardboard carrier that's in her hand. It's filled with three cups from Starbucks, and one's marked with my fave: a large vanilla latte with Splenda and extra cream.

"Thanks." I accept the huge coffee and take a sip. I don't really buy into her reasoning that I need the caffeine, since it definitely isn't going to calm me down. But maybe it'll give me a shot of energy that will make me so buzzed I'll be all excited to go into school. On the other hand, it's only caffeine, not magic.

"Where's Noah?" she asks. "I brought him one, too." Of course she did. Coffee with a shot of espresso, extra sugar, extra cream. The same drink he had every single day this summer, when the three of us worked together at Cooley's Diner, but we always brought in our own coffee because the stuff at Cooley's tastes disgusting. (Cooley's Diner coffee = mud, only, like, more bitter and tinged with the taste of a dirty cup.)

"Noah?" I ask, trying to keep my voice light. My hands tighten around my coffee, and I almost spill the whole thing all over myself. "I dunno." I shrug, like Noah hasn't even crossed my mind, when, of course, he's the only thing I've been thinking about.

"Didn't you guys drive to school together?"

"No."

"Why not? You guys drove to work together every day over the summer."

"Not *every* day," I say. "And besides, I have a car now." I run my hand over the steering wheel of my new car, the car that took me all summer to save up to buy. It's red (perfect), four doors (perfect), a 2005 (adequate) and has 120K miles on it (not so perfect, but beggars can't be choosers, especially when it comes to transportation.) "And besides," I add, "Noah drives to school with Ava usually."

"Oh, right." Lacey wrinkles up her nose. "I forgot that *Ava's* back." She says "Ava" like it's a dirty word. "Sorry," she says. "I know she's your friend."

"That's okay." If Lacey thinks I'm acting weird, she doesn't say anything, which is a good sign. If Lacey doesn't realize anything's going on, maybe Ava won't either. And if Ava doesn't, maybe Noah won't. And that way we can just forget everything that happened this summer, especially what happened last night. Just push it all under the rug and start fresh. La, la, la, there it goes, like some kind of garbage being taken out to the curb, poof! I start to feel a little better. Maybe everything is going to work out after all. Of course, I don't want to be the kind of girl with a scandalous secret, but sometimes you have to take what you can get and just —

Suddenly, something slams into the back of my car, and my whole body flies forward, my chest hitting the steering wheel.

"Shit!" Lacey says. Her fingers tighten around her coffee and the lid goes flying off, her cappuccino sloshing over the sides of the cup and splattering the front of the glittery silver tank top she's wearing. "Shit, shit, shit!" She swivels her head around, strands of her hair whipping against her face.

I look in the rearview mirror. A red car (something expensive—maybe a Lexus?) has backed into me, and the driver, a girl wearing camouflage capris (doesn't she know those are so five years ago?), comes rushing out of the driver's side, and then peers down at my bumper. She looks like she's about to burst into tears.

I close my eyes for a moment, and then open my door and climb out, Lacey hot on my heels.

"What the hell is wrong with you?" Lacey demands. She pulls the sunglasses she's wearing down off the top of her head and slides them over her eyes.

"Oh my God, I'm like sooo sorry," the girl says. She's younger than us (probably a sophomore?) and she twists her hands into a knot in front of her. Her face is getting all scrunchy, like she really might be about to start crying.

"It's okay," I say, kneeling down and inspecting my bumper. There's a tiny scratch, about two inches long, running down one side of it. "It looks like it's just a small scratch."

"A *small scratch*?" Lacey yells. She bends down and looks at the car. "You know how much small scratches cost to get fixed, Hannah? Like thousands of dollars!"

"I'm so sorry," the girl says again. She's wearing Converse sneakers, a black tank top, and about three million pounds of black eyeliner.

"It's okay," I say. She's obviously one of those gothy girls who, like, pretends she's over everything, but inside is about five seconds away from crying constantly. Seriously, goth girls cannot handle anything.

"My dad is going to flip," Goth Girl says. "He just got me this car. For a birthday present."

"Oh, God," Lacey says. I'll bet she's rolling her eyes under the sunglasses, thinking of the hours and hours we spent this summer behind the counter at Cooley's, sweating under the broken air conditioner and serving bottomless cups of coffee to the old men who would come in every day, sit for hours, and then tip us a dollar.

"Look," I say to the girl, before Lacey can tear into her again, "Can you just give me your insurance information?" I guess that's what you're supposed to do in these situations. I mean, I'm not completely sure, since I've never actually been in a car accident. Until a few days ago, I never even had a car.

"Right," the girl says. She heads to her car, rummages around in her glove compartment, and comes back. She carefully copies everything down onto a sheet of paper from a brand-new black binder that's covered with stickers of bands I've never heard of, then rips it out and gives it to me.

"Thanks, Jemima," I say, glancing down at her name on the paper. Jemima? No wonder she looks so nervous. With a name like that you're probably used to bad things happening to you. Starting, of course, with your parents naming you Jemima.

"Why were you pulling out of a space, anyway?" Lacey asks. "School's about to start. Shouldn't you have been pulling *into* a space?" She looks down at the coffee stain on her tank top. "Does your insurance cover clothing? Because this tank top was extremely expensive." It's a lie, of course. Lacey got that tank top for $12.99 at Old Navy.

"I forgot something," Jemima says, chewing on her bottom lip. "At home. So I was going back to get it. And I'll pay for your tank top. How much did it cost?"

"I hope your dad's, like, a lawyer or something, being able to afford that fancy car. Because, honestly, if I get whiplash or some kind of neck affliction . . ." Lacey rubs her neck, ignoring Jemima's tank top offer.

"Okay, well, bye!" I say to Jemima, shooting her a look that says, *get the hell out of here if you want to save yourself.*

She scampers away obediently before Lacey has a chance to threaten any more litigation.

"Lacey!" I say. "You didn't have to scare the poor girl."

"Sorry," she says. "But Hannah, you have to be tougher on people. What if we were pushovers, and she decided to, like, commit insurance fraud or something so that she wouldn't have to pay for your car."

"Insurance fraud? Lacey, I don't think that's really—"

"Besides," she says, "*I'm* the one who should be scared. I have a bad neck now probably."

"You do not have a bad neck," I say, rolling my eyes. I walk back toward the car and open the door.

"What are you doing?" Lacey asks. "It's almost time for homeroom. The bell's going to ring in, like, one minute, and I need to see what Danielle Shapiro is wearing. I'll bet she has a fake tan with one of those little heart cutout things. You know, like skanky body art?"

"You go ahead," I tell her. "I'll just—"

"Hannah!" Lacey says. "You are coming into school! Forget about stupid Sebastian Bukowski and his dumb friends. You are sooo over him!" She crosses over to my side of the car and puts her hands on my shoulders. "Hannah, you are amazing. You are gorgeous and smart and you deserve someone way better than Sebastian. He doesn't even deserve to be a passing thought through your brain." She looks into my eyes. "Now, we are going to go into school, me and you, and no matter what happens, I'm going to be right by your side, okay? Nothing to worry about."

"Thanks, Lace," I say, giving her a weak smile. I don't have the heart or the strength to tell her that Sebastian's not even the half of it. That he's not even the *quarter* of it. I don't have the heart to tell her about Ava, or about what happened with Noah last night. And I don't have the strength to argue with her. So when she takes my hand, I don't protest, and when she pulls me across the parking lot, I force my feet to march in the direction of school.

Here goes nothing.

LAUREN BARNHOLDT is also the author of *One Night That Changes Everything*, *Two-way Street*, and *Watch Me* for teens, and *Rules for Secret Keeping*, *Four Truths and a Lie*, *The Secret Identity of Devon Delaney*, and *Devon Delaney Should Totally Know Better* for tweens. She lives in Waltham, Massachusetts. Visit her at laurenbarnholdt.com, follow her at twitter.com/laurenbarnholdt, and friend her at facebook.com/laurenbarnholdt.

TWO HEARTBREAKING AND GUT-WRENCHING STORIES ABOUT FRIENDSHIP, LOVE, AND LOSS

HER AND ME AND YOU

Lauren Strasnick

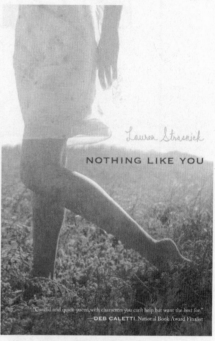

Lauren Strasnick

NOTHING LIKE YOU

"Candid and quick-paced, with characters you can't help but want the best for."
—DEB CALETTI, National Book Award Finalist

Lauren Strasnick

EBOOK EDITIONS ALSO AVAILABLE

FROM SIMON PULSE
PUBLISHED BY SIMON & SCHUSTER
TEEN.SIMONANDSCHUSTER.COM

THERE'S A FINE LINE
BETWEEN *bitter* AND *sweet*.

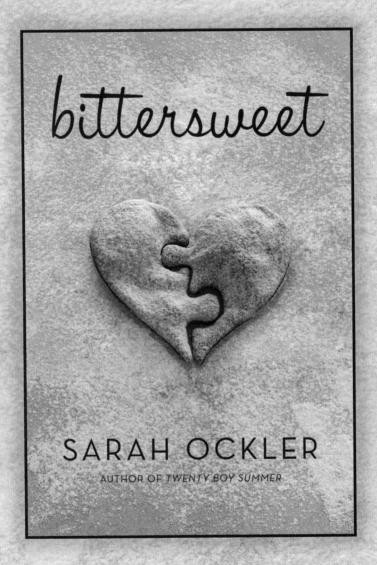

bittersweet

SARAH OCKLER

AUTHOR OF *TWENTY BOY SUMMER*

siMONTeeN

Simon & Schuster's **Simon Teen**
e-newsletter delivers current updates on
the hottest titles, exciting sweepstakes, and
exclusive content from your favorite authors.

Visit **TEEN.SimonandSchuster.com** to
sign up, post your thoughts, and find out what
every avid reader is talking about!

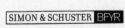